Polishing Saber
Darragha Foster

BLURB: *Polishing Saber* is not your average vampire tale. No Carpathians. No dark, brooding, deadly handsome men out to give you the ultimate hickey. *Polishing Saber*'s vampire is one of the Old Ones—kin to the Hidden Folk in Icelandic mythology. Shape-shifters, too, they have protected their homeland for millennia from insidious witches wearing dead man's trousers. The Necropants. Flayed from the skin of a corpse, steeped with magic runes and foul desires to control, usurp and bring unhealthy changes to Iceland, the Necropants have a will of their own. Including the need for their wearer to consume blood. Though well-hidden for centuries, the Necropants have been found. An Old One has awakened. Big business is planning the utter destruction of Iceland's pristine wilderness. And Saber Evangelista holds the key that all three forces wish to possess.

Dedication: For Thordur Bjorn Sigurdsson

THIS TALE IS A COMPILATION of Icelandic folk legends, actual historical events, and sheer flights of fantasy on my part. I hope the Hidden Folk don't mind too much. – Darragha

Polishing Saber
Darragha Foster

Prologue

Gisli cursed under his breath at the opening of the clay tomb found buried in a niche in the cliffs by an eiderdown gatherer. It was a remarkable find. One with dire consequences. He had long rued the day; he'd wished for it never to come. He had thought the item well-hidden. He had been entrusted to preserve it as a reminder of the great war between the Hidden Folk and the witches as it stood as a silent memorial in hopes that such wickedness would never live to serve and control humankind again.

The Old Ones, Gisli included, had grown complacent, and even arrogant and vain believing that they had ridded the world of men and women from the fabric of evil.

The moment the warm hand of the down gatherer touched the clay sarcophagus, Gisli awoke from his long sleep and realized his dreams of a secure homeland were false and misleading. The ever vigilant, but rarely combatant Hidden Folk, called him to action. He was responsible, thereby he was charged to put right the situation.

He, himself, had sealed the baked earthen box and witnessed in silence as volunteer Hidden Folk transported it and hid it deep inside the basalt of Grimsey. They had sacrificed their lives to the sea after that last great act to protect the secret. Only Gisli remained—and he went into deep hibernation.

Four hundred years passed. Time, tide, wind, and rain had eroded just enough of the crypt to make it the perfect place for eider ducks to nest and leave behind their soft, highly sought-after down.

The man who found the box didn't know what it was—but knew enough to phone the Museum of Sorcery and Witchcraft in Hólmavík, a small fishing village in the western fjords. It was no coincidence that said museum had been founded so far off the beaten track. It had been built upon the epicenter of witchcraft in Iceland. In the lands sacred to the Hidden Folk. In the lands coveted by developers.

The curator was a man of great cunning and abilities—some of which ran toward being quite unethical and unholy. Gisli had followed the man's career in vivid nightmares, and feared him.

The box was hoisted from the cliffs and laid out on the grassy expanse overlooking the bluffs. A tent was erected. Outlined in black against the off-white heavy canvas of the tent, Gisli watched the curator's shadow quiver as the lid was lifted from the box. It was a devil's dance. The curator writhed like a serpent ready to mate entranced by the scent of a female.

Gisli's stomach heaved and he vomited. The curator made his guts churn with rage. The man's sadistic penchant for items of macabre significance preceded him. He would know exactly what had been unearthed. He could read the runes, recognize the spells. He was a man who would break sacred seals without stopping to consider his actions. The curator had once excavated the grave of a Catholic priest at the site of Iceland's first church. Make that *graves*, plural, of a Catholic priest, *singular*. When Protestantism swept Iceland, that last medieval

Catholic priest was beheaded. Adding insult to grievous injury, his head and body were buried separately, in unmarked sites outside the churchyard.

The curator hadn't considered the consequences then, either. He made a spectacle of his find and subsequent reburial of the priest in a new crypt. His fascination with dead things frightened some, and intrigued others. Most were simply embarrassed that a learned man would seek out sensationalism and greedily disturb the spirits of the land for publicity or profit.

Gisli choked as a photographer's flash popped. The canvas tent brightened with each snap, like caged lightning. Each flash heightened Gisli's rage, fear, anxiety.

The curator had opened an Old Icelandic Pandora's Box. Only Hope would not remain, no matter how quickly the box was closed. Hope lay in one place only. In the utter destruction of the treasure.

A collective gasp rang through the tent, echoing to the perch where Gisli sat with his gyrfalcon brethren. A shifter, he could hide in plain sight as a gull, a tern, a puffin, or as the mighty raptor, gyrfalcon. An ancient being of vampiric origin, he didn't need to see with his eyes to discern the activity inside the tent. He could smell the foul odor of death and taste it on the air. *Nábrók*, the heinous dead man's trousers, wrought in human flesh and emblazoned with staves of great power, had been found.

And now comes a witch to claim them, Gisli thought. *And now comes the battle for Iceland.*

Chapter One

The condom broke.

Her granny down in *N'Awleans* had always told her to look in little things for signs and wonders of God's plan for her. Saber took the fall of the Trojan empire as a definite sign she should get out of town.

Everything in her life had been pointing that direction for some time, anyway. The death of the mighty Trojan warrior during the heat of battle was the last straw.

She'd had her fill of strong coffee and hot men. Goodbye, Seattle.

The process of relocating halfway around the world had given her time to clear her head and purge her soul of vigorous men with members larger than *Trojan-Enz* could handle. That's what she got for taking home a guy from the *Dog and Pony Show*, a rather risqué singles club on First Avenue. She'd taken home a man built like a horse, twice as smelly, and just as full of manure. Never go grocery shopping when hungry and never go to a sex club when horny.

Saber had lived abroad for two weeks, and hadn't had a roll in the hay for six months. Sister Saber Evangelista. Saber the celibate. Saber the born-again virgin. Celibacy was not for her.

She'd stopped sleeping. Awake, her mind racing, she more than once caught herself fantasizing about getting some. It wasn't the orgasms she missed. Those she could get on her own, thank you very much. She had what it took to bait the hook. She liked to think of herself as Rubensesque—a healthy, attractive fleshy woman with lots of curves and a mind so sharp it could out cut Wilkinson Swords.

She'd hooked her share fair of lovers. Sometimes he'd flop around her deck and sometimes he'd be a trophy catch. Her fishing hole had been well stocked, but had become much too predictable. Enter the *Dog and Pony Show*.

Saber didn't feel she was promiscuous—just active. She didn't bed every man she met, after all. Thereby, she'd made it six months sans a tumble without having to resort to chewing on car tires to calm her nerves.

The itch had returned one bright evening as she lay awake staring out the window into a landscape of stark and barren beauty—and she figured it was time to find someone to scratch it for her. Her new home had some prime pickings, too. No need to rush things and bed the first reasonably agreeable suspect. The tease of going without was almost as stimulating as the act itself. She'd wait until just the right man came along. And if he turned out to be the boy next door, well...*yummy*.

She had a lucrative consulting contract, the envy of her peers and associates, and more money being socked away into her 401K than she could ever spend in one lifetime.

Saber Evangelista was the backbone of AlumaTrends, mistress of their IT Department, and developer of the very software the company had just banked on to make it appear their projects in virgin lands were environmentally friendly. *Appear* being the key word.

Saber had developed Ice-Eye to map more deeply and more thoroughly than any other GPS device, and any given government, ever had. Ice-Eye promised to locate and map the areas of least impact in delicate regions such as Iceland where one false step of the drill could open up a geyser in the middle of a multi-billion-dollar project. In truth, and it was a truth she conveniently ignored, Ice-Eye's deep viewing capabilities could be used to find precious metals such as *gold in them thar hills* and map out, to the smallest detail, exactly how much land could be chewed up, swallowed, and spit back out during the mining process before international treaties and moral codes of conduct were broken. Turning a blind eye to the rape of Iceland wasn't too hard with as much money as they were throwing at her. Of course, maybe that's why she hadn't been sleeping, too.

She held the passcode to activate the system. She held the *only* passcode.

She'd made the system impenetrable, hacker proof. No wonder she'd been courted by government agents from three countries. Governments didn't pay enough. Private industry was where the big bucks were. There'd be a meeting soon—a meeting when she would sign over the passcode and her association with the company would end. First, she had to train the hard-hats and novice AlumaTrends techs to use the system she'd written. Then she'd sip champagne with the suits, get her picture taken at a ribbon cutting, and drop out of the picture. Twenty-six years old and retired. Make that twenty-six, retired, voluptuous, active, and smart. Very smart.

She'd developed a modern day *Enola Gay*. It wasn't the bomb, itself, but the mechanism to deploy the thing. It promised to make a handful of AlumaTrends execs very wealthy.

Saber was both the beauty and a geek. A dangerous combination. She told folks she wouldn't date outside her IQ range, no matter how much those execs with their mid-one hundred seventy IQ's begged. She was a gorgeous, intelligent woman of color in a world of pasty white men who rarely saw natural sunlight. And she knew that she was their queen.

THE HAIRS STANDING up on the back of his neck told Gisli the *Nábrók* had not yet left Akureyri. The sweet summer air carried a foul undertone—a scent no human could detect. It clung to the air like a heavy, invisible mist. An air-freshener gone rancid. It was the foul magic of the Necropants working its insidiousness on a greedy witchling.

He'd been awake for nearly a week, reeling with the knowledge that the Necropants had been both rediscovered, then stolen. It took some time for him to track them after they'd been scurried off Grimsey by rats in mens' clothing. He blessed the names of all that was holy that the soulless, devil-beget item had not yet left Iceland. He had risen from his ancient slumber like a phoenix and grew more powerful with each passing day as the sun remained high in the sky longer and darkness never came. He was a vampire. And a shape-shifter. Like his kind had done for centuries, he embraced the light and flew in the bright skies of the midnight sun as a falcon. Like all vampires, he needed blood to live. Warm blood. Living blood.

His search for the stolen Necropants had kept him too busy to feed. He was starving. He needed to find a suitable donor. He needed to create a helper-being from mortal clay by taking his or her blood and imparting unto that person new thought processes. A human liaison to act on behalf of his hidden realm. A Renfrew to his Count. But without the bugs.

He'd circled the village on his bike, feeling his way around the townsfolk, hoping one of them would fit the bill. It was easier to prey on sheep. Sheep had no hidden agendas to be mastered, opinions or blood tainted by power and greed. Too bad he needed to utilize the services of someone farther up the food chain. If he gave into the hunger, he would lose the ability to enlist an ally of the human persuasion. One chance only—so his choice had to be wisely made.

It was her scent that alerted him. Her enticing, contradictory aroma of powerful innocence and blind intelligence wafted about his head on an icy north wind like an errant feather. It tickled. She had a tantalizing bouquet of wantonness and virtue combined with a touch of darkness. Like an exotic perfume, it announced her arrival long before she appeared. She was jasmine in the air, gingered-chocolate on the tip of his tongue. She'd been in indirect contact with the Necropants, too. Their scent pervaded her aura. Through her blood, he could track them. And destroy them once and for all.

He set off on his bicycle, hoping to catch her eye without divulging too much of himself in the process. He needed her to develop enough interest in him to come meet him on his turf. Curiosity may kill the cat, but it creates allies, too.

The sight of her took his breath away. She was his opposite. Where he stood blond and fair and purely, regally Icelandic, she strolled dark and exotic—a fascinating contrast in a land where dark eyes could stop traffic.

Though far from human, he had a man's needs—and watching the uniquely dark beauty wandering the streets of Akureyri made him acutely aware of those needs. When had he last taken a woman? He couldn't remember.

Maybe that was about to change.

AS HORNY AS SHE WAS, it was no wonder she reacted to the blond god's reflection in the shop window as if she was a teenager worshipping a rock idol. Took on a whole new meaning to window-shopping.

Icelandic men, overall, with their fair complexions and wind-kissed ruddy cheeks and blue eyes, were quite enticing. This guy she wanted to consume right then. Right there.

Her cheeks flushed. Her heart began to pound; her temperature rose. That naughty place between her legs tightened and throbbed.

Their eyes met in the reflection as he sailed by on his bicycle. He shot her a sly smile and nodded his head. Saber had to avert her gaze. He was magnificent. Perfect. If the beauty of a moon reflecting on a pond took human form, it would be he. How could any human on the face of the earth be worthy of looking into this man's eyes? He was *divine*, in every sense of the word. Clad in a light blue sweatshirt emblazoned with the words GRIMSEY TRUST on the back, he sailed down the slope into the ferry lane. He then stopped and looked back at her before drifting out of sight onto the loading dock.

She had hoped he would stop for her. She was getting used to men stopping dead in their tracks when passing her.

That had pretty much been the case since moving to Iceland. Being a woman of color in as shallow a gene pool as northern Iceland's, was proving to be a worthwhile change of venue. An exotic mix of Korean and African American descent, Saber had been living and working in a society that could trace its genetic make-up back to eleven hundred fair haired and complexioned settlers.

Two weeks on the rock and she'd marked seven notches in her lipstick case. Seven times she'd smiled politely when approached, fumbled through short conversations of combined Iceland and English, but hadn't taken a gent up on an offer of drinks yet. Truthfully, that boy next door was still looking pretty damned good that way. Still, she was biding her time. However, if this guy had just stopped she'd have made an exception.

She frowned in his wake. *I just saw an angel. I swear to God, that man is a freakin' angel. Angels aren't supposed to make you feel this way!* The gruel scene in the musical *Oliver!* came to mind. *Please, sir—I want some more.*

Saber sighed, having lost interest in the antique books in the shop window. She wanted to flip through the blond's pages. He'd disappeared on the five o'clock ferry. Good thing, too. Or she might have tried to catch up with him, tackle his bike, and do the nasty with him on the gutter side of Laxagotta.

Dismayed and a bit chilly in the ever-present northerly breeze, she set out for home, which was painfully all uphill. Up a remorseful, steep hill. Only intrepid Icelanders would have planned that Akureyri, Iceland's garden city, be situated on a hill. A thousand years ago the settlers to the area didn't care about the problem of wearing heels while shopping. They'd probably been thinking about the fabulous natural harbor and defensible location. Silly Vikings.

Red-roofed blue and purple trimmed stucco houses dotted her path, tucked neatly inside little fenced-in yards where dwarf evergreen trees stretched to catch the long rays of daylight. Little fences where behind good citizens lived peacefully; the most exciting event in their lives was watching the flowers grow in the midnight sun.

The walk was long and excruciating, made interesting only by thoughts of the blond god on the bicycle.

The elderly couple she'd taken a room with were very quiet with limited English skills. Saber was fairly certain all the English they knew came from watching "The Simpsons" during the dark season—as the government shut down television during daylight months. No Homer during June, July, or August. A true travesty.

Saber communicated with her landlords via her rudimentary Icelandic vocabulary, the teenaged neighbor with his blue ribbons in speaking English, German, and Danish, and her translator app with its Icelandic/English/English/Icelandic dictionary.

The octogenarian couple at Freyjugata five had rented her a room with a private bath. She had never seen two people use more table sugar or drink as much coffee.

Each meal was accompanied by *skyr*, a thick yogurt hand-mixed by the wife and blended with heavy cream, and of course, sugar. Definitely an acquired taste, though it was easily recognizable and by far the least foul-smelling item in the fridge.

The couple never slept—which worked for Saber, as neither did she. No Icelanders slept too long during the summer. Twenty-four-hour daylight saw every Icelander up all night, drinking coffee. How anyone worked productively during the summer months was beyond her. The banks in Akureyri closed at one o'clock every day for their employees to take a "sun coffee" break for thirty minutes. It was not unusual to see bank tellers in their skivvies sitting along the sidewalk outside their place of employment, a soft-drink in one hand, cigarette in the other, basking in the sunshine like proud cats.

Saber looked forward to St. John the Baptist Day, when it was perfectly legal to roll naked in the morning dew. Authorities around the country turned their heads on public nudity that morning as long as no one was touching someone else's nakedness in the grass.

She made a mental note to find and get to know the blond with the bike before St. John's Day. There'd be a morning worth waking up for!

Two or three months of the midnight sun followed by nine months of darkness was their lot, those genetically pure Icelanders. Saber had long loved their history, myths, and legends. Her family didn't get it. Her mother, the Korean daughter of an ambassador to the United States, had married a Black military officer with political aspirations. They had tried to interest her ethnic studies and politics. They'd become resigned to the fact that their bi-racial daughter had interests as dissimilar to her background and upbringing as was humanly possible. They shook their heads as they walked by her room when she still lived at home. Pictures of Viking gods and books on Leif Eirkisson just didn't match their dream for their daughter. Sure, they were a combined-race family with ties all around the globe, but Saber had fixated on the one thing they weren't. *Nordic.*

When an opportunity arose to travel to Iceland for her company, Saber jumped at the chance. Of course, it could have simply been an emotional reaction to the bursting of the dam after riding the wild pony. Iceland offered her a chance for a fresh start and a shit-load of money. God knows she didn't want to show her face around downtown Seattle anytime soon. She'd taken home a *pony boy.* She needn't be reminded of her poor choices.

For her, Iceland was the opportunity of a lifetime.

Beautiful place.

Beautiful people.

Yummy men.

A second chance.

The job provided housing and a one-year work visa. It was her idea to board with the elderly couple. Exposure to the culture and all. She couldn't very well do that living alone in a small flat.

Kristjana, her house mother, the Frá—pronounced 'frow' as in eye*brow*, was enjoying a bit of sun coffee on her back porch when Saber trudged up the hill to the little red house with its four-foot high evergreen trees planted by the front stoop. Kristjana had been a very famous actress in the Icelandic theater during her youth. At eighty-five, she didn't look or act, old. Must have been all the caffeine and sugar.

"Jaeja," the old woman sighed under her breath as Saber collapsed onto the porch.

"Jaeja," Saber replied. It wasn't a word of greeting. It was more of an Icelandic *oy vey*, pronounced *yie (as in tie)-ya*. Saber sat up and glanced over the fence and as politely as she could tried to tell Kristjana that she was heading over to the neighbor's. "Eg vil fara til Steinrikur's heim." She knew the words were right—it was the order she said them in and the conjugation of the verbs that was way, way wrong. The old woman just smiled and nodded.

Saber replied with the word for thanks, as she headed "over the hill" to the neighbors'. Another Icelandic colloquialism—the neighbor's house was not next door, but over the hill—even on level ground.

Kristjana muttered something she didn't understand. Icelanders often spoke with a very breathy accent, making those not accustomed to the language think the entire nation was asthmatic. Not so, of course. The quiet manner of speaking was just their way. Until they were drunk. Then things could get loud.

Saber passed through the garden gate between her home and the neighbor's. "Rik?" she called.

The large, youthful redhead opened his bedroom window. "Hallo, Saber. Need to find out what that funky purple sauce in the Frá's ice-box is?"

Saber laughed. "How did you know?"

"I could smell it. Kristjana made pickled cabbage today. I'll tell you this—when you see something bright purple in an old Icelander's cooler, don't eat it," Rik warned.

"Can I come in?" Saber asked.

"Of course. The front door is open," Rik replied.

He was a good kid. Eighteen, intelligent as all Hell and she was pretty sure, had a hard-on for her. Thing was, she was terribly attracted to him, too. Firm young Icelandic flesh at its best.

His parents weren't home.

Dare she enter the bedroom of a European boy? Sixteen was the age of emancipation in Iceland. This boy was out of school, two years into junior college and just about to transfer to the university. Fair game. A little romp with the boy wouldn't be illegal—though she was an older woman. But then she might end up with having him hanging on her when she wanted to spend a bit of her free time digging for angels.

"How are you, Ricky?" she asked. They exchanged a bear hug, lingering for a moment in each other's arms before nervously pulling away. There was nothing remotely right about the way Saber felt when in his arms, however briefly. She was pretty sure Rik felt the same titillation as she did. He always gave her a little extra squeeze. She could feel his tension—it was smack dab front and center. It was naughty bad—this attraction. Bad in the best way possible.

Rik beamed, obviously enjoying his Americanized nickname. "I am fine. I am studying to write a paper for the Center."

Still in his arms, Saber looked up into the boy's eyes. Bright, bright, clear blue eyes framed by gorgeous unblemished skin and deep red hair. Her little Viking. He had some height and weight on her. She wasn't small at five foot eight and one hundred seventy pounds. She was voluptuous and enjoyed her full figure. Rik was easily six five and maybe two hundred fifty pounds. All of it worth the effort to unwrap.

She leaned back, allowing his embrace to cradle her. Her arms were suspended around his neck. He dropped her onto his bed.

Saber laughed and sat upright. Crotch level. *Damn.* "What's your topic?" she asked, hoping to deflect some of the pounding sexual tension between them. It was going to happen. It was—and they both knew it. It was just a matter of when. Every time they visited, it got harder and harder not to make one move farther up the sexual intimacy scale.

"I am writing of Akureyri's ghosts," Steinrikur replied.

"Ghosts?" Saber laughed. She reclined onto her elbow on his bed box. The hand-carved nature of his bed told her it had been in his family for generations. The thin, firm mattress puffed out a loose eiderdown feather as she settled onto the bed.

"There are many in our history. I wrote about the Necropants found on Grimsey quite recently," Rik replied.

That caught her attention. "Necropants? *Dead* pants?"

"Yes." He popped a mint into his mouth and offered her the pack. "It is only the second *Nábrók* to have been found intact. A very rare and exciting find. However, after they were removed from Grimsey," Rik paused. "You do know about Grimsey, yes? The little island above Iceland that is over the Arctic Circle?"

Saber took a mint. She sounded out the new Icelandic word. "*Now-broke.* Is that right? I do know about Grimsey, yes. Bird Island."

Rik smiled. He certainly was a handsome young devil. Maybe she should do the boy and see how thing go. Put a smile on both their faces. She cast her eyes over the fly of his jeans.

Looks like the boy has a healthy package—but the thought of riding another pony gave her chills. Too big was too much. She wanted *just right* like Goldilocks.

Rik continued, "*Wery* good, Saber. Your Icelandic improves each day. Any way, after they were put in the museum, they were stolen. It was not unexpected, however. *Nábrók* were once highly sought after. Witches in Iceland used to dig up the body of a man to flay the skin from the lower half to make breeches in order to become *draugur*. A special symbol was sewn onto the," he touched his hand to his crotch, "the *hrtspungur*."

"The balls?" Saber replied, knowing that *hrtspungur* was a particularly nasty dish made of pressed pickled ram's testicles.

"Yes, the balls. The symbol would bring coin into the purse, and give the wearer very special powers."

"Such as?" Saber asked.

"Strength. The ability to walk in the clouds. And a very long life. But……the wearer had to consume blood to keep the magic strong. The Necropants need fresh blood. The Old Ones hid the Necropants to stop the *draugur* from becoming too powerful. There was a war."

"Who are the Old Ones?" Saber asked.

"The vampires, of course," Rik replied.

Saber smiled. He pronounced it *wampyr*. Very cute. "There was a war over who could drink blood? God, Rik. In Iceland that can be accomplished by eating dark rye!"

"They could not eat their blood in their bread as we do when we have *blothmir*. It had to be fresh. Sheep or human, mostly."

"Wearing the Necropants made the witches vampires? The witches became vampires?"

"Not vampires. They are separate beings. The witches who wear Necropants and feast upon blood are called *draugur*. We use the same word for ghost in Icelandic. To an outsider, it could be confusing. The witches and the *draugur* are not the vampires here. The others—the Old Ones—are the vampires. I must add, too, that it is the Necropants, when worn by a witch, that require the blood. To stay warm and like natural skin. They are spell-crafted and have a life force of their own. If the witch does not drink blood, the Necropants will dry up and wither away, and turn the witch's body to ash."

Saber swallowed hard. "Lovely."

"We do not dismiss the fanciful so quickly here. As I said, the Necropants have been stolen. And many sheep have been found dead without their blood recently. It is believed that a witch has stolen the Necropants to become a *draugur*. He or she is now feeding in order to gain strength, wealth, and power over the elements. If a *draugur* walks again, then too shall an Old One—in order to recapture the pants and destroy them forever. If there is one, there is the other. They are two sides of the same coin. I have always been more in favor of the *draugur*. They bring change to Iceland. I do not believe their motives are evil. When last the *draugur* worked the spells, Iceland became a Protestant country. The mindset of our Protestant leaders brought sweeping changes to the country over a two hundred year period. It changed things here for the better. The Old Ones are self-appointed guardians of the land—but they do not relish changes to their home. They will protest, and there will be a great battle between the creatures."

"Are you telling me that there's going to be local news coverage of a war between the witches and vampires?"

"It has been recorded in our history that such things took place. *Draugur* appear when great changes need to occur. They are the harbingers of change to the land. The vampires are angels bound to Iceland by magical fetters and prefer to leave things as they have always been."

Angels? I saw one, I think. Saber interjected, "Magical fetters? Like the rope made from the sound of a cat's footfall and spittle of a bird that tied up Fenris the wolf in Norse Mythology?"

Rik nodded. "Yes, exactly. The *wampyr* feed only to live and do not kill, though through the taking of blood from a human they become like a shadow to that person's soul. The host shares a body and spirit with the *wampyr*. They can make the person act on their behalf. There are stories of Old Ones, or their followers, leaving sheep, sod, or driftwood at the doors of starving families. There are stories of women receiving deep sexual pleasure at odd times—such as during Mass, because she is possessed by an Old One and he has chosen that time to make love to her—from the inside out! The vampires are regarded as good beings—beings of light—though I have my doubts. Some truth about them was long hidden. My father excavated a rune stone—the Husavik bowl... "

Saber nodded. "Yes, I read about that. Quite a find."

"When translated, the runes told the true story of the Old Ones and their war with the witches. Someday, this new information will enlighten Iceland. With my father's assistance, I am researching all known historical aspects of the witches and the *draugur* quite intensely. With a copy of the fully translated Husavik bowl, I shall prove who truly is the source of evil in Iceland. It will be a prize-winning essay."

"From what I've heard, the evil of Iceland is the aluminum plant and the developers building it. My employers. Me."

Rik nodded and replied in Icelandic, "Fortunately for you, perhaps, I am one of the proponents for the project. Iceland needs jobs for its young people other than the fishing industry. After University, I shall be a journalist and shall report on the great doings of Saber Evangelista and AlumaTrends. Of course, many are very concerned with the impact of the plant. The location is sacred, and has long been said to be home to many *Huldufolk*. They say the Old Ones will not allow the rivers to be dammed and land flooded to generate power for the smelter. The *wampyr* owe a life-debt to the *Hidden Folk* for sacrificing their own to hide the Necropants. Moreover, the *Huldufolk* are sworn enemies of the *draugur*."

"I am amazed that Iceland's mysticism blends so readily with its modernization. But I wonder, Ricky...why not tap the tides or divert more geo-thermal activity to power the plant as opposed to damming a river and flooding acres and acres of land? This is Iceland! Geysers open up in farmer's potato fields here. Energy is not an issue. I've asked the same question to the head honchos of the company and they look at me like I'm an idiot. Just teach the hard-hats how to use the computer system, Miss Evangelista, or we'll slap your ass behind a desk where glorified geeks like you are should be."

"I have no answer, either—though slapping your ass does sound lovely." Steinrikur winked. "The people are divided upon this issue. Some want great modernization and offer their family lands to the power companies. Others fight like true warriors to protect their property and keep foreign developers away."

"Spoken like a true warrior, yourself, Ricky. Now, about slapping my ass..."

"You know, Saber—I like you *wery* much," Rik replied.

Saber smiled. She loved his "v" words. *I like you wary much, too. Now take off your jeans.* She bit her lip. "I like you, too."

As though the gauntlet had been thrown; the glove slapped across the cheek—the call to duel had been made. At the *Dog and Pony Show*, such words could easily be translated to mean, *I want to wear your butt as a hat.*

And then there was silence.

A rather pregnant aura of need, want, and desperately hot passion filled the void between them. Saber had been there a time or two before—but never with a younger man—even when she'd been his age. She let her eyes fall to his fly again. She then cast her eyes upward. He was smiling at her. A subtle smile. A smirk.

She needed to break the tension between them before she followed her gut, reached out and...

Saber straightened her back, sitting more erect and less in a "come hither recline." "My, it's getting hot in here." She hesitated, again finding herself apprehensive about a little May/December sexual tension. Delightful, sweet tension. "It could be how utterly distracting I find you, but I'm not sure I understand what you're telling me here," she paused, almost wishing she hadn't said that. She caught Rik's smoldering eyes fixed on her bosom. *Yeah, I distract him, too.* "All righty then, Ricky, before we continue heading the way I think we're heading..."

Steinrikur pulled off his over-sweater. Saber swallowed hard at the outline of his young, muscular chest through the plain white t-shirt underneath.

She continued, slowly unbuttoning her own sweater. "Make that the way I *know* we're heading. Necropants found recently on Grimsey have been stolen. It is feared that witches who wish to gain certain magical abilities have stolen the gruesome drawers, which get hungry of their own accord." She ran her hands across the soft cashmere of her sweater, over her breasts. A big tease. And she knew it. "Sheep have been killed and drained of blood—and with no true predators in Iceland, the deed is being blamed on witches donning the Necropants in an attempt to harness the magic and become all powerful, to stop the Iceland's indigenous pixies and trolls from halting the construction of the power plant and smelter in the western fjords. Assisting the pixies is at least one fallen vampiric being, who does not feed indiscriminately, but who acts like an agent for the Salvation Army in times of famine, and may be of divine origin."

Her sweater hung open, revealing that which God and Grannie gave her. An ample bosom encased in a Wonderbra.

"It sounds better when explained in Icelandic. It would start something like this: *Tunglid vedur i skyjum*—the moon wades through the clouds. And I have not even told you the entire legend yet," Steinrikur replied. He knelt before Saber and pushed aside her soft lavender cashmere sweater. He pulled it over her shoulders. "We still believe in hauntings here. It is not uncommon for people to seek advice from a witch before breaking ground for a new house, lest the Hidden Folk are disturbed. Trolls and fairies live here, Saber. Why not vampires?"

Saber took a deep breath. The anticipation was killing her. *Take me now. You are the brightest, most intelligent, most articulate eighteen-year-old boy I've ever met and I want to rock your world.* "Fascinating."

With more experience and finesse than his age dictated he should have, Rik smoothly slipped Saber's bra straps down. "I am sure you are not here to discuss my article. Do you need an interpreter next door, my love?"

Saber smiled. It was common to refer to a friend as a loved one. It didn't mean he was in love with her. Actually, he probably was. She figured they were about to shag quite fiercely. And quite frankly, the thought of running her breasts across that thick red mane of his... Whoo! "I came to ask the best way to get to Grimsey. But now, I think maybe I need to ask you something else."

Rik lowered his lips to Saber's. "And what would that be?"

"When are you going to go *íviking* on me?" she asked, referring to the Norse Age custom of young men leaving home to seek adventure, fame, and fortune.

Rik pressed his lips to Saber's. He climbed atop her, pinning her to his bed. She shifted her weight a little and returned his kiss, running her hands through his thick red hair.

Like teenagers rolling in the back seat of Daddy's car, they mashed on the bed, hips gyrating and hands exploring. When they got naked, Saber didn't know. All she knew was that she was hot for this kid. Smoking hot.

She reached between them to get a grip on his erection. She had a pretty good idea of its girth by the weight of it on her leg.

She liked what she felt. As soon as her fingertips touched the head, she wanted to taste it. Taste eighteen-year-old boy flesh.

Saber laughed and rolled Rik off her. As he ran his hands over her, she spun around on the bed and took the tip of his penis into her mouth. He was already hard, engorged. She stroked her hand upward on his shaft and pumped the head against her tongue.

She wiggled and writhed as he explored her vagina and clitoris with his soft fingers. She suppressed a cry of *Alleluia!* when he lifted her onto his face.

Doing a sixty-nine egged Saber on. No woman ever forgets how to give good head—it's like riding a bicycle. She got her rhythm down, pushing up with her hand and going down with her mouth, swallowing as much of him as she could. He was no horse—but in Iceland, ponies were the norm. This guy had nothing to ashamed of.

His moans told her that he liked her mouth on him, and she sure as hell liked what he was doing to her. She thought she might drown him with how wet he was making her. Those little flicks of his tongue upward onto her clit, man...the boy had talent. Saber had to give his dick a rest and relax her head against his groin as she felt the surge of orgasm building between her legs. This was the moment she had long anticipated. The call for safe sex. The momentary eye of the hurricane before passing into the storm. "Rik," she whispered. "We should use protection."

"Just fuck me, Saber. I'm a *wirgin*," Rik replied before burying his tongue in her anus.

"And I know I'm clean." She could barely get the words out. Her eyes rolled back in her head as wave of pleasure swept through her from stem to stern. Anilingus. Forbidden; naughty; nasty. *Damn, he's good.*

She pulled forward and in one swift move, impaled herself on Rik's hardness, going for a reverse cowgirl position. He brought his knees up. She reclined forward and used them to balance herself as she slid herself up and down against his shaft.

This was what she had been missing. Six months of celibacy came to an abrupt and sweet conclusion as she came. She bucked against Rik so hard the bed creaked and threatened to collapse. He pushed up into her in orgasm moments later.

Still entwined, Saber rested her head against his knees. He stroked her lower back. After-glow set in. She squirmed a little, enjoying the sensation of his still-hard penis inside her.

"Saber," Rik whispered.

"Yes?"

"I want you again."

Saber sighed. "I can tell."

"Let's go out to the Jacuzzi. My parents won't be home for hours," Rik said.

"What if I scream when I come?" Saber asked.

"This is Iceland. Women screaming in orgasm is a common occurrence here."

Saber pulled herself away from Rik. It was painful, this knowingly brief but still too long a separation of penis and vagina. Her clitoris throbbed, calling to her, *gimme more of that!* Such is sex with a teenaged boy. *Happy, lucky me.* "Before I lose consciousness or the ability to speak—before I'm completely fucked-out, I'm wondering, Rik, shall I fly or take the ferry to Grimsey? I want to take my bike."

Rik laughed. "You should take the ferry, of course."

"Know the schedule?" Saber replied.

Rik replied as they walked nude through Rik's house and into the backyard. "The ferry leaves Akureyri at eight o'clock in the morning and returns to Akureyri around noon, then departs for the island again at five. On Grimsey, if you cross the Arctic Circle on foot, the priest will issue you a diploma and pierce your ear."

Saber mouthed the words *pierce your ear*, and considered the actions of such a priest, but held her tongue.

Iceland's most abundant natural resource, hot water, awaited them in a lovely blue glass block Jacuzzi. She melted into Rik's arms as she followed him into the hotpot.

"Would you like me to accompany you? To Grimsey?" he asked.

"I'll have a little adventure. I'll be all right."

"Enjoy Grimsey. But Saber, do use caution. The spirits of Iceland thrive in isolation. Grimsey is as far north as you can get without having to paddle on an ice-flow. And take a lunch with you. I have not heard good things about the pub there. With only a hundred people living on the island, the services are very limited."

Saber nodded. "Flatbread, smoked lamb, and a thermos of coffee. How does that sound?"

Rik smirked. "I would prefer Dairy Queen."

Saber wrinkled her nose. *I guess teenaged boys, hot or not, have garbage guts.* "Even using Icelandic beef and sans the additives abundant in American fast food, I have no plans of ever walking into any restaurant where they ask me: *can I help the next one down here, please?*"

Rik laughed. He cupped Saber's breasts as they floated in the bubbles. "Then I shall take you to *Perlan*."

"Darling, I don't think even Bill Gates could afford dinner at the *Pearl*," Saber replied. "It's only the most exclusive and expensive restaurant in Iceland. Maybe even northern Europe! And it's on the other side of the island."

"I won a prize for writing a very good paper on the mail-order brides from Thailand and the Philippines comprising five percent of Iceland's work force. They are taking over our public market. I won dinner for two at the Pearl. The daily news ran the story. Would you like to see a copy?" Rik's voice grew low and soft. "I have been coming into some money, lately. Such as young Icelandic men don't usually see."

"That's quite the generous prize. *The Morgunblathid* forked the bill?"

Rik wrinkled his lovely brow. "Forked?"

"American slang. The newspaper sponsored the prize?"

"Yes."

"You don't want to take one of your friends?"

"No. I would rather take you."

"So when's dinner?" she asked. She stroked his penis with her right hand and lifted herself in the water so that she was facing him. With one thrust, he'd be in her. *Come to mama, baby boy.*

"I am working tomorrow night with my father, but the day after—how would that be? I shall make an appointment for us." Rik carried Saber to the opposite edge of the Jacuzzi and slid into her.

"At the Pearl. In Reykjavik?" Saber asked.

"Of course," Rik replied, giving her one good thrust. For an untried boy, he sure knew how to screw. His movements were deep and slow and with each pass, teased her clitoris from its sheathe. Saber wrapped her legs around his hips and held on for dear life as his thrusts grew more vigorous. He pressed her against the stone wall of the Jacuzzi so hard she knew she'd be bruised in the morning, but there was no stopping the juggernaut of lust moving him. She forgot about her back a moment later as she achieved a second stellar orgasm.

Water whipped out of the tub as they thrashed in climax, not suppressing one little gasp, moan or cry. Rik gritted his teeth and arched his back as his orgasm poured into her. He was milking it for every last iota of pleasure. She liked a man who saw things to full conclusion!

Exhausted, they moved to opposite sides of the Jacuzzi and played footsie while allowing the steam and jets to soothe their savage passions.

Rik smiled slyly and said softly in typical Icelandic manner, "Don't forget about me when you catch up with that which you are seeking to find on Grimsey. I know you are seeking something, and perhaps it is just that diploma for crossing the Arctic Circle on foot—but if you don't find what it is on Grimsey, then perhaps it is here."

A very astute comment from a very young man. She might forget about him if she took up with the blond god. She enjoyed monogamy—even serial monogamy. She wasn't good at juggling relationships. If it's Tuesday it must be Brendan or Saturday with Mark. One lover at a time, thank you very much.

Would she pursue firm young flesh or angelic beauty?

The answer rested across the Arctic Circle on a little island with a hundred inhabitants. And she knew it.

AS THE FERRY PULLED away from mainland Iceland, leaving relative civilization behind, Saber realized that she could sum up Iceland in one word. Windy. Never had she traveled to a place where the wind never ceased to blow. The biting chill burned her cheeks as she stood at the bow of the ferry, her borrowed bicycle secured to a steel bollard aboard the deck.

She reached up and twisted her curly black hair into a knot to keep it from whipping her head and giving her whiplash as the force of the boat moving against the wind wreaked havoc on her carefully primped 'do. Her crazy ass African hair with its thick, glossy Asian characteristics was her best feature. That and the startling green eyes. Where those came from, no one knew. Some bizarre genetic trait going back a couple of generations.

She'd skipped eyeliner and mascara before boarding. Good thing—her eyes were getting a good workout from the wind. She'd packed some cosmetic essentials in her backpack, along with lunch, water, and condoms. One should always be prepared, after all.

Her ears were filled with her ear buds. Shakira's "Eyes Like Yours" made her want to dance across the deck. Common sense told her to hang on as the ferry left the harbor and headed out across the Arctic Sea to Grimsey. No dancing aboard a small vessel sailing across wind-tossed waters. Her hips would have to remain stationary this trip.

Grimsey rose up from the Arctic like a green jewel floating atop a smoky glass mirror. Small jewel. Very, very small.

The entire settlement was situated around the tiny harbor and landing strip for the puddle jumper that flew to the island every three or four days. A single radio tower rose in the distance. Probably for cell phones and to transmit data to fishing fleets in the high Arctic. Saber clutched an old tourist map of Grimsey to keep it from blowing out of her hands. She found it tucked in the bookshelf in her room.

A handful of women and small children boarded as she rolled her bike off. Saber parked the bike alongside a pylon and checked the map against the actual layout of the town. Town may have been too big a word. A pub, with a guesthouse, a kindergarten, a post office, and a church. What else does an arctic island three miles long and two miles wide need? A dog sled rental?

Several tidy houses, resembling those in Akureyri, dotted the landscape. Gulls and terns cried, and a single dog barked.

Though it was scarcely eleven o'clock in the morning, Saber thought she'd get a drink at the pub. Probably coffee. Maybe a beer. Who knows? If the angel lived on Grimsey, he might be thirsty, too.

The tavern was amazingly well-equipped for an establishment catering to a hundred year-round residents, the odd pilot, and two or three hundred day-tripping tourists a year. A painted mural behind the bar showed a puffin and gyrfalcon sharing a nest while several ptarmigans looked on. The puffin was sitting on an egg.

"Komdu sæl," Saber said politely.

"How are you?" the barkeep replied in perfect English.

"Oh, you speak English. Wonderful. Could I have a cup of coffee, please?"

"Sugar?" the man asked.

Saber shook her head. "Cream. *Rjomi*," she replied, happy she'd remembered the word in Icelandic.

The barman pulled a dark brown cup from behind the counter and poured strong smelling black coffee for her. "What brings you to Grimsey? We've not had many tourists this season."

"Curiosity," Saber replied.

"There is nothing here save for many birds and of course, the circle."

"Will I get a certificate if I cross the circle on foot today?" Saber asked.

"Yes, and an extra prize if you go across it backward. Today is the longest day of the year and the circle radiates magic this day."

"It is the solstice, isn't it? I'd forgotten. Well, if I follow your advice, what is the extra prize?"

"Walk across the circle backward, and with your eyes closed. Once across, open your eyes, facing the direction you came from. Turn slowly to face the opposite way. As you turn, an apparition of your true love will appear before your eyes."

"I'm not looking for true love," Saber replied.

The barkeep laughed. "Then it shall be the vision of a good time for you. Okay?"

"Okay," Saber replied. "I'm wondering about something."

"Yes?"

"I saw a man on a bike wearing a t-shirt that said GRIMSEY TRUST on the back. What is the Grimsey Trust?" Saber asked.

"Something you will not find in guidebooks, that's for certain."

Saber smiled. "Oh, yeah? Do tell."

"The Trust was founded by emissaries to the mortal world on behalf of the *Hidden Folk,* I'd say, about three hundred years ago," the man replied.

Saber held out her hand. "I'm Saber Evangelista."

"Hakkon Magnusson," the man replied, shaking Saber's hand.

"So, Hakkon, the Hidden Folk have humans doing their bidding?"

"Do you find that hard to believe?" Hakkon asked.

Saber took a sip of her coffee. "No. I find it intriguing."

"Will you be staying the night? The room is available," Hakkon offered.

"I hadn't planned on it," Saber replied.

"I see you are holding an old ferry schedule. There are no more runs today. Maintenance," Hakkon replied. "And your ferry has already departed for the mainland."

Saber shrugged her shoulders. "I guess I'm staying the night. Do you take VISA?"

"Lunch is at two. Dinner at eight. And yes, I take VISA." He passed Saber a key. "Enjoy your night on Grimsey."

Saber downed her coffee. The rich, bitter taste mixed with the sweet cream energized her. "How much do I owe you?"

"Comes with the room," Hakkon replied. "And your meals, and for you, a private washroom."

"Well, so much to return to. Thanks. I'll be back. I'm going to explore," Saber announced.

"That's good. The bar rush starts in about fifteen minutes when the fishermen come in for their second breakfast—you don't want to smell that way all day."

"Thanks for the tip. Anything noteworthy I should see?" Saber asked.

"The manager for the Grimsey Trust is better qualified to give you a tour of our little island. Shall I ring him for you?"

"Sure," Saber replied. "That would be nice."

Hakkon picked up a handset from under the counter and punched in a number. The conversation was so quick she couldn't catch but two or three words. "His associate will meet you at the sign post."

Saber laughed. "Signpost?"

Hakkon made a gesture of direction with his hands as he replied, "The signpost—like in M*A*S*H. It tells you how far to somewhere else. It is at the end of the road."

"I'll see you at four," Saber replied. "Thanks, again."

Hakkon nodded. He mumbled something under his breath that she didn't quite catch. Something like, "maybe."

Maybe he'd see her at 4:00?

Saber hopped on her bike and rode east, the direction Hakkon had pointed her. The sole village on Grimsey was not too lively a place. Bright eyes surrounded by wrinkled skin peered out at her from behind a lace curtain. She got the odd smile from a child playing on a porch. There were no more than twenty or so houses scattered along the single roadway between the ferry landing and the airstrip.

She passed the mercantile and the physician's office and apothecary. By appointment or chance, said a little sign on the door, in English. A joke? There must have been a very slight incline, as she had to peddle faster the closer she came to the signpost. It had a dozen arms stretching out from a concrete-encased base in desperate need of paint. It did remind her of M*A*S*H.

She engaged the kickstand on the bike and hopped off.

"You are on the line," a voice called to her in flawless English.

Saber turned to face the speaker. A very handsome older man with snow-white hair had ridden up silently behind her. "Are you looking for a tour?" he asked.

"Should I cross it walking backward?" Saber asked. She paused for the man to laugh. He didn't. Apparently he didn't know the rules. She put on her business face. "Grimsey Trust?"

"I am only an employee of the Trust. Gisli is its heart. He asked me to give you directions to his home. He lives in a sod house, in the old style—not far from here."

"A sod house? That's interesting," Saber replied.

"You must go across the Arctic Circle to get there," the man replied.

Saber laughed. "I believe I'm standing on the Arctic Circle." She took one step north. "Now I'm across it."

"Ride north from your present location and you will come to Gisli's house. It is the only one of its kind on the island."

"Why couldn't he meet me here, himself?" Saber asked.

"He is watching the ice flow."

"He watches ice?"

"Lots of ice. You'll see. Enjoy your visit."

Saber smiled and took off on her bike, noting that a word scrawled a fork of the signpost said 'civilization'—and it was pointing in the opposite direction.

The moment she left the manicured village on the southern tip, the island's true form became abundantly apparent. It was an open-air aviary. Birds were everywhere. Nesting on rocky outcroppings. Lining the cliffs. Swooping into the black waters for food. Flying in the air above her, doing a strafe and run over her head to sway her away from their eggs or chicks. Bird droppings littered the basalt and cries of gulls drowned out the gentle coos of other nesting seabirds. Not ten minutes north, and so near the edge of the island that she could see land's end, a little sod house with a green grass roof rose up from the red earth. A trail of smoke rose from the round stone chimney. The scent of roasting meat filled the air.

Saber dropped her bike and approached followed a stone path cut straight down until her head was at roof level. A cheerful red door welcomed her. She knocked.

"I'm not at home."

The voice sounded mature, intelligent and deep. Saber turned. She nearly toppled over from surprise. It was her angel.

"Grimsey Trust?" she asked. "I'm Saber. Hakkon at the bar..."

"Gisli. I am the administrator for the Trust. Please, join me. I'm recording an ice flow."

"Why?" Saber asked.

"Why come with me, or why do I record rogue icebergs? I'm teasing. Don't bother to reply. Just come with me. Do hurry." He paused. "We've met, no?"

Saber shook her head and climbed up the stairs, accepting Gisli's hand as she reached the top. She didn't want to look at him. He was too brilliant—like a halogen lantern. She had expected a surge of white-hot electricity to flow from his embrace. His hand was cold. "Your hand is like ice," she commented.

"I've been watching ice. Must be the resultant effect. Come. We can chat while I record my data," Gisli replied.

He didn't release her hand. Dashing off like middle schoolers about to smooch behind the track shed during class time, Gisli led Saber to a rather high-tech viewing post, set up to view straight out to sea.

Saber was already cold. The wind never stopped in Iceland, and Grimsey had zero defense from the chilly North Pole air shooting down from the top of the world. Gisli's touch chilled her to the bone.

"What are you searching for?" she asked.

"Look," Gilsli offered.

Saber put her eye to his high-power telescope. She squinted and focused, then pulled her head away in amazement. "It's a bear."

"Yes, it is. A polar bear on an ice-flow. I have alerted the authorities that they should make haste and rescue it before it dies. I'm sure it is very hungry and very thirsty. It is a young male."

"Did it get lost?" *A stupid question. How would he know?*

"Grimsey has seen polar bears drift down on ice before when the summer is very warm. It does not happen too often, but this year, we have seen two. The first bear was very old, very large. He must have stayed alive for quite some time while he drifted. Alas, his thousand-mile journey did not end well, for he came to Grimsey too late. This little bear, however, I think the fleet will rescue him and return him home to a more solid ice shelf."

"The ice is melting. Global warming," Saber replied.

"Yes. And I watch for the bears as they are the symbol of Grimsey and I respect them dearly. But you did not come to listen to me speak of bears. You have come to learn more about Grimsey, yes?"

Saber nodded.

"Are you a bird watcher?" Gisli asked.

Saber shook her head. "Not really, no."

"I do not suppose you have a fascination with fishing in cold waters, then?" Gisli asked.

"No."

"Then how can I help you?" Gisli asked.

"I want to know about the Necropants." She didn't. She came to find him, and here he was and now, for perhaps the first time in her life, she wasn't sure what to do with her lure. Reel it in or let it bob on open waters?

"Ah, you are a witch!" Gisli teased.

"No. I'm just curious," Saber replied.

"*Nábrók* are not for the curious. I think you came to see something else on this island," Gisli replied.

Saber choked. She tried to pull her hand away. He wouldn't allow it. "Oh, really? What makes you think that?"

"I saw you, too, you know. You, with your hair and skin and eyes like a moonlit night. In the reflection of the shop's window you looked like a mirror image on a calm, dark sea." He held up her hand to his lips and kissed her knuckles. His kiss brought a tingle of warmth to her fingertips. "Be truthful with me. You came because you wanted to meet me. It took me almost ten minutes to get your attention, riding back and forth on the street. I wanted you to notice me. I invited you here."

Saber tried to pull her hand away.

He shook his head. "No, dear one. Your hand is mine. Soon enough I hope you will give me more than just your hand, too."

Holy Mother of God this man is smooth. "Look, I admit it—I came here looking for you. I saw you get on the ferry and, all right, you are really attractive. I do want to get to know you. But Gisli, aren't you moving a little fast?" Saber replied.

"Grimsey makes men hard and honest. Brutally honest. It is our way. I say to you now, I want you—and I think you want me, too."

Casual sex on Grimsey? This is what I wanted. This is why I came. Come on, Saber. This is the opportunity of a lifetime. Screwing a blond god across the Arctic Circle. "I did—I do. But..."

"Do not allow yourself to be swayed by fear and false morality, Saber. It dulls your shine."

"You wanna polish Saber, huh?" Saber asked.

"I see years of misuse have dulled your shine, Saber. There is perhaps, even some rust on your soul. A Viking likes his weapons honed and ready. Well-oiled, with a clean, sharp edge."

"I've got my grandmother's round corners, darling," Saber replied. "Not much sharp about me except for my wit."

"Your curves may be the most dangerous weapon I've polished to date."

Saber smiled. Her hand had grown warm in his. "Right here? In front of the polar bears?"

He pulled Saber in and lightly ran his lips across hers. It wasn't a kiss. It reminded her of how a cat feels its way with its whiskers. He buried his mouth under her chin. His embrace felt commanding and powerful.

"I like your style, Gisli, but I don't even know how you like your coffee yet," Saber said, stifling a satisfied sigh as Gisli kissed her throat.

"You know how I like my coffee. I like it sweet, like the taste of your flesh against my lips," he replied.

"Yeah, but you don't even know how I like my eggs," Saber said. "In the morning."

Gisli took a deep breath, holding Saber's curls to his nose. "You like your eggs scrambled. Beaten with heavy cream, black pepper and dill."

"Good guess," Saber replied. She extended her neck and head to allow more room for Gisli's whiskery kisses.

SHE KNEW SHE WAS STEPPING out of a frying pan named Rik and into a fire named Gisli. What did Rik expect from her besides sex? She'd have to put an end to it before it went any further if she was going to take up with this man of radiant perfection. She didn't want to turn this guy down. She'd crossed the damned Arctic Ocean to screw him. They both knew it, too.

The blonde god was one smooth son of a bitch. Saber had been courted and wooed and sought after by men all her life. Black men, Asian men, white men. Even some women had tried their hand at getting her into the sack—and one of them successfully—but never had she been swept off her feet and out of her right mind as quickly as she had been by this white-blonde Icelander with his brilliant blue eyes and funky sod house.

She entered the house by having to duck her head under a driftwood lintel. The outward appearance of Gisli's home screamed rustic, cold, drafty. She expected to see lambs grazing atop the grassy roof as they approached it, and hear their soft bleating while inside. The living quarters were astonishingly bright, cozy, warm, and modern.

"Oh, my God," Saber exclaimed as she entered the main room. "This place is huge."

"It is. And I am using only half of it for my home. The cavern was excavated by troupes of King Olaf Haraldsson of Norway in ten twenty-five. He very much wanted a military presence on Iceland. His builders settled in by hollowing out a small cave connected to a lava tube. They constructed this smashing little fortress inside the vestibule."

"Is this the best-kept secret in all of Iceland?" Saber asked. "This is incredible."

"I have modernized it, of course."

"You have satellite communications equipment. Christ,—and a microwave. Yours is the first I've seen since I got here."

"I have Internet access, television channels from all over the globe, and yes, this is a very well-kept secret. One you are obliged to hold sacred, as well."

"Are those Norse shields?" Saber asked, pointing to the pitched corners of the ceiling line.

"Replicas of the originals, alas. An earthquake damaged much of the original building materials. I salvaged what I could and did some retrofitting, you might say."

Saber walked around the comfortable room. A small fireplace in the center glowed softly—and the smell of roasted meat enticed her to seek its origin. "You have a roast in the oven."

"Lamb shank. Very tasty. And potatoes. Will you join me?" Gisli asked.

"No one makes beef pot roast around here, do they?" Saber replied.

"Beef? In Iceland? Surely, you jest. We have sheep—and many of them. It has another hour to cook. Do you think we can fill the time?"

Saber sat down on a decidedly IKEA-esque chair. "What about your polar bear?"

Gisli unzipped his windbreaker and pulled off the hoodie he wore under it. "He doesn't like lamb. They eat fish. A Norwegian fishing vessel is on the way to save him, anyway." He stripped off his basic white t-shirt, revealing a very well toned, if not very white, very smooth chest.

"Look, Gisli...I'm flattered," Saber began.

Gisli knelt over her and silenced her with a kiss. "You should be."

He kissed her throat while his hands went to the soft folds of her sweater over her breasts. "You have beautiful skin. You are perfect. Like the midnight sun," he whispered. "I have never made love to a woman of color before. What do you call yourself?"

Saber shivered as his fingertips caressed her nipples over the smooth black wool. She forced a single word reply from between her lips before finding his mouth pressed against her mouth once again. "American."

Gisli dropped to his knees, taking her to the floor with him. He rolled atop her, straddling her, the weight of one of his legs atop her. "You are a melting pot of true American beauty. I could worship you."

He kissed her again. Then returned to the teasingly sensual nuzzling of her throat. She felt a slight pinch above her left clavicle. "Nibble nibble little mousey," she giggled. "You're a biter, huh?"

He didn't reply. Except by using firm, quick hands to strip her of her clothing.

Of course, she helped. She'd come to Grimsey do him, after all.

An almost nightmarish sequence of images passed before her eyes as they made love. Floating in fog. Buoyant. High. *Am I drugged? Did he drug me?* Her mind was one place and her body was responding in another. Disconnected. She felt disconnected from herself. But every time she tried to speak, she found her mouth closed by lips, tongue, fingers, or penis of Gisli, the god.

She lost track of time. She barely recalled where she was; who she was. She willed herself to relax and enjoy the slow, deliberate motions of his groin to hers. That's when she noticed that, somehow, as he was doing her, he was also flicking at her clitoris with his tongue. It wasn't his dick inside her. It was a dildo. *He's using a dildo. Kinky.* She pondered the sensation. *No. That feels like the real deal down there.*

The flicking against her clitoris continued. *Damn. Boyfriend knows the drill.* She moaned. All wafting about in time and space came to an abrupt end as he pulled her down to earth, centering on that little bud between her legs. The place that was about to go nuclear.

He chuckled as Saber sighed and gripped at the arms of the chair. His head was at her shoulder. His lips were on her shoulder. *The freak is biting me! Oh, my God. Damn! Each flick of his tongue against the base of my throat feels as though it's happening way farther down the pike. In fact, a few more strokes like that last one and I am going to ...*

Explode in a breath-sucking, body clenching, full-on, full-force orgasm.

Saber wanted to curl up into a ball as the first wave of pleasure hit. She envisioned curling into a fetal position because it hurt so damned good. He just kept thrusting and flicking and thrusting and flicking and there was no time to breathe as a second surge hit. She struck his shoulders with her hands, hoping he'd move away or come or something!

A hot knife into butter, man. This guy was doing her like a hot knife through butter. Last thing she knew, she'd melted. Someone come dip a lobster tail in her 'cause she'd been drawn and served.

SABER AWOKE DRESSED and alone, her cheek pressed against a Formica tabletop. A little puddle of drool had formed, and the hand her head had rested on was wet, and asleep.

"Good morning. You know, the beds here are much more comfortable than the tables."

Saber lifted her head and squinted to discern who dared speak to her through the pounding fog of a headache she had. "Hakkon? What the Hell am I doing here?"

"You wandered in last night, sat down with a pint and fell asleep. You looked so sweet with your curls in your beer that I left you," Hakkon replied.

Saber stretched and stood. "I feel funky."

"Your sweater is misbuttoned. And where is your left shoe?" Hakkon asked. "Did you fall over a cliff on your way to meet with the Trustee?"

"He pushed me, I think," Saber replied. "Do you have some coffee?"

"He's quite elderly. I doubt he'd have the strength to push you over a cliff. Perhaps you came to close to a tern's nest and were startled. It has happened, you know. You did not try to gather eider down or steal a puffin's egg, did you?"

Saber approached the bar, finding each movement difficult and the very act of thinking painful. She took the steaming mug of coffee and drank.

"You are bleeding," Hakkon said softly.

Saber lifted her lips from the rim of the cup. "What?"

"Your shoulder. You are injured. Here, allow me to help you." Hakkon lifted the hinged flap on the bar's top and came around to Saber's side. Without asking permission or washing his hands or displaying his first aid card, he pulled Saber's sweater down over her shoulder. Though she tried, she could not crane her head enough to see the wound.

"Well?" she asked.

"You have been punctured in two places. The blood is not fresh. You do not recall falling?"

"That son of a bitch bit me," Saber cursed.

Hakkon frowned. "Hallo? You were bitten?"

"Yeah, by a snake in the grass," Saber replied.

"There are no snakes in Iceland," Hakkon replied rather matter-of-factly. "You wash your shoulder. I'm going to get some moss."

Saber took another sip of coffee. *Moss? He's getting moss?*

She slid off the barstool and behind the counter. Using a clean bar towel, she washed off her shoulder. It stung like a mother.

Hakkon walked back in a moment later. "This is Icelandic purple moss. It is full of natural healing. Pack it on the wound. I will use some cloth to bind it. In a day, you will be healed." He passed a handful of wet purplish moss to Saber. She palmed it against the puncture wounds at the top of her clavicle.

"You keep the stuff outside your front door?" Saber asked.

"In Iceland there dare five hundred forty-five types of moss. Grimsey is home to more than seventy varieties. It grows naturally. Even outside my door," Hakkon replied.

"Thank you. Hey, you said the Trustee was old?"

"In his late eighties, I believe."

Saber helped herself to another cup of coffee. "Does he have a grandson? Maybe a great-grandson, about thirty years old?"

Hakkon shook his head. "I don't think so. He has a personal assistant, Jon. He no doubt met you at the signpost. The Trustee rarely leaves his home these days."

"The sod house?" Saber asked.

Hakkon laughed. "A sod house?"

"Yes, built into a natural cave along the cliffs..." She could see that Hakkon was ready to burst. "No sod house. Right?"

"There are cliffs if it makes you feel better. We have excellent cliffs. Some of the best in all Iceland. But there are no sod houses on Grimsey. At least not for centuries."

"I didn't fall, Hakkon. I'm pretty sure I didn't fall. Is there a set up on the north side of the island to watch for polar bears?" Saber asked.

Hakkon choked on his own cup of coffee, the black nectar spraying outward as he laughed. "No, dear one. We don't watch for polar bears. They arrive sometimes, but we don't set a plate for them."

Saber rubbed her eyes. "When's the ferry?"

"An hour ago."

"Crap!" Saber cursed.

"You can take the plane home. I secured you a seat. You can make a deposit into my account for payment."

"Thank you. When does it leave?" Saber asked.

"Finish your cup and head to the landing strip."

"Where's my bike?" Saber asked.

"You arrived last night without it," Hakkon replied.

Saber looked at her shoeless left foot. "And my shoe?"

Hakkon shrugged. "You had quite an adventure, didn't you? I hope, in some way, your curiosity about Grimsey has been quelled. Perhaps Prince Charming will find your shoe and return it to you."

"Right." Every muscle in her body ached—and made that fact acutely known to her as she tried to tidy herself up a bit before dragging her sorry ass to the landing strip. She pulled back her curls and twisted them into a bun, and straightened her clothing. "Do I look like the wild man of Borneo or am I socially acceptable to get off the plane in Akureyri?"

"You look as though you battled a *draugur* and lost."

"Draugur. A ghost—or a witch with the unholy powers of *Nábrók*. Perfect."

Hakkon put a large hand on Saber's arm. "Draugur are great liars. They hide in plain sight. They blend themselves to match their victim's life. Do you know how to recognize a draugur?"

Saber laughed. "Whomever it is that lives in the sod house and spends his time watching for polar bears, is real. I have the bite marks to prove it. I think he was a *draugur*." Saber took a quick inventory of her body. She didn't feel as though she'd participated in rough sex. She'd been *there* a morning after or two, and this wasn't one of those days. This was far more confusing—but definitely not a day of post-coital *hurts so good*. "How do I recognize one, Hakkon?"

"Their breath. It smells sulfuric when they wear the Necropants. You must look for the mark on their hip. Like a brand. It is a runic symbol. Some modern witches have it tattooed on their left hip. In the past it was carved into the flesh or burned in. A brand."

"I doubt I'm going to see an unclothed witch and get close enough to smell his or her breath any time soon."

"Sometimes we choose our bed partners unwisely, no?" Hakkon laughed. "No matter. You are leaving us now and will stay away from witches with bad breath. All right?"

"Thanks. I think I'll head back this way, however. I've a sod house to find."

"You look for your ghost-house, my dear. When you find it, I shall get a license to rent it out to German tourists."

"I'll talk to the owner for you. I think he likes me," Saber replied.

"And how do you know that?"

Saber pressed her lips together, wondering if she should reveal her encounter. "He made love to me. Kind of."

Hakkon smiled. "Yes, this explains much."

Saber put her hands on her hips, feeling much like a defiant teenager. "I'm not crazy?"

"No, you are not. I think you ran into the den of a Hidden Folk. They have a way of playing with a person's mind. I, myself, have not served one of their kind in my pub for years," Hakkon replied. "Others on Grimsey live have developed uneasy accords with them. I do not make bargains with trolls and gnomes. I just serve beer and hand out the room key to guests."

"The young guy—the Grimsey Trust guy—" Saber began. "May have been a pixie?"

Hakkon laughed. "A pixie? No, perhaps not—but *Huldafolk*, nevertheless. A good story for your children someday, no? About how you came to watch birds on Grimsey and were tricked into relations with a mystical being."

"Yeah, there's one for the supper table. Look, thank you. I'm sure we'll meet up again. My work schedule allows me quite a bit of free time."

"What is your business?"

"I'm a trainer for AlumaTrends. I'm really nothing more than a glorified computer technician."

"For the company planning on changing things in the western fjords. I see. It is no wonder you were seduced by one of our elemental beings. It is said they are banding together to put a stop to the plant, you know."

Saber nodded. "I've heard that."

"You will be out of a job soon," Hakkon whispered.

"A good geek can always get a job. Goodbye, Hakkon. And thanks," Saber replied. "Bless," she added, using the traditional Icelandic phrase when parting company.

Hakkon didn't look up from his barware. "Bless."

Still missing one shoe, no doubt looking quite disheveled and feeling ridden hard and put away wet, Saber dashed to the landing strip. The plane was loaded, ready and waiting. Plane? It was the size of a tinker toy.

"Hakkon's guest?" the pilot confirmed. "What happened to you?"

Saber shook her head. "Don't ask."

"Did you cross the circle?" he asked.

"Yeah, I did." She looked around her nervously. It was a four-seat, itty-bitty airplane, which didn't look sturdy enough to jump a puddle much less an expanse of the Arctic Ocean.

Before she could react, the pilot grabbed her head and secured her left ear between his index finger and thumb. A moment later he pushed a needle through the lobe above her other piercing. She suppressed her initial knee-jerk reaction to avoid having the pilot's strong grip rip her earlobe in half. "What the Hell was that for? Is the needle clean?" she yelled. "I was told the priest did the piercing, and I didn't see him today!"

The pilot laughed. "I am the priest, and now you are a *wiking*. You have crossed the Arctic Circle on foot, and thereby, receive a mark. It is tradition. You can have the goldsmith in Akureyri re-pierce it for you. And yes, the needle is clean. I use them only once." He passed Saber a box of tissue.

Holding a tissue to her ear, not sure if she should say thank you or bitch-slap the guy for assaulting her, Saber hunkered down into her seat and prayed that the plane would make it to Akureyri. She wasn't ready to meet a polar bear on an ice flow face to face.

RIK VIDARSSON BOTH loved and feared the man he still called "Pabbi," and always strove to stay in his good graces. Sometimes, when a dark mood came upon his father, which was not such an easy task. He'd learned that his father's word was law. No discussion. Only obedience.

Still, Rik trusted his father. A great bond of father to son existed in their lives and for his father to harm him or give him bad advice would have been both shocking and traumatizing. So, when his father announced they were taking a country drive, Rik did not question his father's motives. "Pabbi," he began. "I have a date tonight. We are so far out, so far away from Akureyri. I have concerns. This is the night I shall take the Cessna to Reykjavik."

His father remained silent. He parked the car and bade Rik exit. The drive had taken them to Lake Myvatn—Mosquito Lake. Myvasveit was an area alive with bugs, sheep and volcanic activities of various natures. As they crossed the sulfur field, Rik could not help but wonder what his father was up to.

"Steinrikur," his father replied. "I need your help with a project. My greatest discovery to date lies just ahead."

"I am honored, of course, Pabbi, but would not one of your research assistants be better qualified to assist you?" Rik asked.

Vidar Gunnarsson, curator, archeologist, and blackheart, turned to face his son. "I need you."

"Yes, sir," Rik replied.

"Tell me of your date," Vidar commanded as he and Rik gingerly maneuvered through the hard-baked earth around the bubbling sulfuric mud puddles.

"It is Saber. Our new neighbor."

"A beautiful woman. She is American. And older," Vidar replied. "You must use caution when with an older woman, son."

"Too late for that, father," Rik replied.

Vidar laughed. "My boy has become a man, I see. Well, this is good timing, for what I need you to do requires a man's strength. Do not become too attached to Saber, however."

Rik followed behind his father, fighting off the swarming gnats as they left the mud pit into an expanse of green calderas surrounding the area around the still-active volcano, Askja. Sheep nestled in the green shelves caused by millennia old lava flow. They watched with disinterest as Rik and his father trudged by.

"It is not too much further ahead of us, son."

"This site has been thoroughly excavated and explored. I cannot imagine that anything of value remains in this place, save for its stark beauty. What did you find?" Rik asked.

"The Husavik runic bowl told of a spot here, near Krafla, at the base of Askja, where magic seeps up from the earth like a geyser. I found that site. It is quite impressive."

"Magic? Real magic?" Rik asked. "Is it guarded by the Hidden Folk?"

"I have not seen one, but I think it is an outlet to their realm. The fumes seeping from the ground make me ill and I cannot breathe the vapors without suffocating. I am, for all my degrees and honors, not worthy."

"And you believe I can?" Rik asked.

"I do."

Another half-mile and Vidar stopped. "It is there. Just ahead. I have marked the area with a stone circle. You must enter the circle and wait for me there. Remove your clothing first."

"Remove my clothing?" Rik asked. "What is this, Pabbi?"

"Do not disobey me, Rik. This is your path. Why you were born."

"My destiny is to stand nude in a stone circle in a grass covered lava field teeming with gnats and sheep?" Rik asked. "I have been thinking journalism was my vocation all this time."

"Go," Vidar commanded.

The tone of his father's voice alarmed Rik enough that he obeyed without further questioning. He stripped and walked toward the stone circle, swatting flies away from his privates.

There was nothing uncommon about the ground under the stone circle. It was grass. It was grass surrounded by stone and sheep dip, as were most of Iceland's wilderness areas.

Though sheltered from much of the wind by the mounds, Rik shivered from the cold. "Father!" he called. "I am freezing. May I dress?"

"No. Not yet." Vidar emerged from behind another mound, naked and holding something quite carefully in his arms. Something leathery, very delicate and thin.

"What have you there, Pabbi?" Rik asked.

"Put this on. You will be warmed by it," Vidar replied.

Rik took the leathery item from his father. His stomach heaved as he recognized the shape of a lump on the front side. It was very clearly, a penis. Or what once was a penis. "Nábrók? Pabbi? Did you steal the Necropants from your own museum?" He didn't want the things in his arms, but knew better than to drop the extremely valuable artifact to the ground. "I am going to be quite ill. Please, take it away from me."

"Put them on. I assure you, they will not tear and they will fit you perfectly, as if they were hand-tailored for you."

"Pabbi, I do not wish to hold this insidious item, much less wear it."

"Do it." Firm. Decisive. Unquestionable.

Rik retched as he donned the unholy breeches. He forced stomach bile back down his throat. It burned, making him gag all the more.

The ancient human flesh leather made his skin crawl. His hands began to perspire. Though he stood in a cold draft barely circumvented by lava pinnacles and earthen mounds, he began to sweat from a fever brought on by pure anxiety.

He coughed and choked, spitting to the side and breathing through his mouth as he slid the Necropants up. They did, indeed, fit him like a glove. It felt disgusting.

Eyelets on the left side held sinewy straps for securing the breeches. He couldn't bring himself to tighten them.

"Why, Pabbi? Why make me wear these inhumane trousers?" Rik asked. He nearly leaped out of the circle as the ground under his feet vibrated and steam gently rose from the grass. It wafted about him, warming him.

"Stay inside the circle, Steinrikur. Stay inside the circle until I tell you to leave. No matter what happens." His father knelt outside the stones and lit a cigarette.

"You don't smoke, Pabbi," Rik said softly, feeling fuzzy and lightheaded—almost unable to vocalize his thoughts.

"I am sorry for this, but it is necessary," Vidar replied. He took the cherry-red end of the cigarette and touched the tip to his son's hip just above the unlaced closure of the Necropants.

Rik screamed, but found himself unable to move. The steam had encased him like an iron maiden. The pain was excruciating. He could smell his own flesh burning under the touch of his father's cigarette.

"Be still," his father commanded. "The stave must be wrought perfectly in your flesh." He looked up into his son's red eyes. "I'm sorry, Steinrikur. The pain will soon end."

Rik tried to glance down, to show his father his tears, to view his charred flesh. The smell was overpowering. He could not move his neck. Tears streamed down his cheeks, but still his father continued the offensive, impossible act.

At last, Vidar stood. "It is done."

"Why? Why Pabbi?" Rik sobbed.

Vidar walked away, disappearing again behind a mound. He returned with a leather flask. "Drink," he commanded.

Desperate to please his father and be released from the magical bonds holding him, Rik took a hard swig of the liquid from his father's flask. It was warm, thick and salty.

Rik vomited red blood. "You feed me blood, Pabbi? Why?"

"Wait for it," Vidar replied. "You will be healed."

Rik gasped as the pain of the burns on his hip vanished and the disgusting corpse flesh trousers melted into his body. Suddenly, very suddenly, he understood. "I remember, Pabbi. Long ago, the journey to the western fjords..." Rik bowed his head. "I had forgotten." He knelt inside the stone circle. "I am the son of witches. We have a mission. How could I have forgotten these things?"

"The truth was hidden from you for fifteen years. I knew it was time to open your heart to your past when you began researching our kind in such diligent fashion I thought you'd find mention of your own grandfather is a *draugur* tale. We are the *draugur*, Steinrikur. And now, our most sacred artifact is returned to us and is worn, by you, our prince." Vidar placed his hands on his son's head. "You are my son and heir. You are the binding tie and stave of progression of the *draugur*. You are the destroyer of those who would oppose us. This is what you were born to do. You are the witch-child of darkness."

Rik stood. "I remember, Pabbi." He wept. He remembered all too well.

"Yes. The memories of your childhood initiation. Do you recall the pledge you made to walk with me in all things? To do my bidding as both your lord and your father? Do you recall how to kill our enemies by tricking them into killing each other? These things you were taught long ago."

Rik nodded. "I do."

"Nábrók spoke to me when I first I touched them. The spirits of all *draugurs* from time immortal pressed me to awaken you. Time to rally you to the cause. We must not allow progress to slow. The men who come with their Euros and dollars to our land are pawns we must utilize, move, and control for our benefit. Do not allow the construction of the dam to be stopped. The waters will flood the homes of our enemies and we will rule the western fjords once again. But be wary...an Old One is awake and seeking Nábrók. He has found his ally with humanity, too. And you have a date with her. Tonight."

"Saber has been kissed by an Old One?" Rik asked.

"He smelled Nábrók on her because of my association with you, and lured her into his embrace. I cannot wear *these* pants in this family, Steinrikur. It is up to you to be a man and a witch, and bring the wealth of many nations to the western fjords."

"Teach me what I must do, Pabbi," Rik replied.

"She must die."

"She won't like that," Rik replied.

Vidar shook his head. "Think, carefully, Steinrkur. Do not make light of this situation or attempt to shroud it in any way with humor. You must grasp the truth of our kind. She must die. I wanted to wait until she had handed over the final codes to AlumaTrends, but now that she has been seduced by an Old One, she must be dealt with immediately." He handed his son the flask. "Drink."

Rik cringed. "It's blood."

"Sheep's. Yes. You must consume it to keep Nábrók happy. They appear as your flesh when well-hydrated. Do not let them wither, or you will turn to dust with them."

"Happy pants?" Rik asked. "Pabbi, please remember this is the twenty-first century, not the tenth. Happy pants sounds so superstitious in nature to be almost comical."

"Magic has no boundaries in time or space. What was magic in the tenth century is magic now. You don't want to make Nábrók unhappy. Look where you stand. You stand on the entrance to the underworld and are surrounded by Satan's own breath, you drink the warm blood of a sheep and plan the demise of our enemy. Magic is strong in Iceland. The *draugur* are strong because of it. Drink. Now."

Rik lifted the flask to his lips. "It is disgusting." He spat red after swallowing. "Pabbi, I thought Hekla was considered to be the gateway to the underworld, anyway. It is much more of a romantic tale than a stone ring at Myvasveit surrounded by sheep dip. And Pabbi, I like Saber. Is there no other way?"

"Medieval folklore would have the world believe Hekla is the key, but it is not. The runes on the Husavik bowl tell a different story. I found this vortex from their directions to it, but could not enter it. It wanted *you*. So I say now, to you, the chosen one, it is better to drink the warm blood of a sheep than to have Nábrók suck the life out of you, starting with your penis. So, drink well and often, and do not test me with stupid questions."

Rik took a hard swig of warm blood from the flask. He shuddered as he forced the thick, chunky liquid down his throat. "I am burned with a witches' mark?" he asked.

"I have marked you with the stave of the Necropants. All witches bear a mark. It was necessary," Vidar replied.

"And so is the death of Saber Evangelista," Rik replied, a single tear rolling down his stained face. "I am saddened by this turn of events in my life."

Chapter Two

Saber felt like she'd been through a rock tumbler as she stepped off the puddle jumper. No wonder Rik had told her to take the ferry. Arctic winds vs. late-model four-seat airplane. No contest. Wind wins.

Bruised, sore, and feeling stupid as hell for not knowing exactly what happened with Gisli, Saber took a taxi back to the house.

She hopped into the shower, planning to clean up and take a nap.

Oddly, the moss had helped heal whatever the hell it was she'd done to her shoulder. The marks were clear, however. Two puncture wounds graced the flesh of her clavicle. Yeah, he'd bitten her. Saber pounded her fist against the bathroom sink. Bite marks meant tests and more waiting periods to see if she'd contracted Hep or HIV. No...Iceland has very, very low incidences of STD's. *Unless he's been putting the bite on every damned tourist, I'm probably all right. Better find a doctor to test me, anyway. Jesus Christ. What do I say? Hi, I was molested by a pixie who took a bite out of my shoulder. Can I have an HIV test, please? Fuck.*

She wrapped a red bath sheet around her and stepped out of the steamy bathroom.

"Well, don't you look handsome," Rik said.

"Hi, Rik. I didn't hear you come in," Saber replied. She wasn't surprised to have someone enter the house without knocking. After all, it was Iceland.

"I saw the taxi drop you off. Did you find what you were looking for on Grimsey?" he asked.

Saber walked into her room. Rik followed.

She held the towel tightly around her. "Would you mind if I get dressed?" she asked.

"No, I don't mind." Rik smiled.

I have a damned puppy dog on my heels. "I meant in private."

"Do you have something to hide from me, Saber?" Rik asked.

"Yes. Many things. Now, please step out." She waved her long fingers toward her bedroom door. "Come on, Rik. Give a girl a break."

"What happened to your throat? On your collar bone?" Rik asked. "Did you injure yourself?"

"I did. I went over a cliff, lost the bike and one of my shoes, and was subsequently attacked by gulls which pecked these holes into my shoulder."

Rik approached Saber and ran his fingertips over the bruised, torn flesh. "They look like bite marks to me."

Saber coughed. Rik's body odor smelled rank. "You been working out or something?" she asked.

"I'm sorry. I know, I need a shower. I went with my father to *Haverarond* and I have not yet washed."

"No wonder you smell like hard boiled eggs. Hanging out in sulfuric mud pits will do that to a person," Saber replied.

"I'll come by at six o'clock to take you to dinner. My father's pilot will take us," Rik said.

Saber glanced at her alarm clock. "Pilot? You were serious about going to the Pearl? In Reykjavik? I thought we were just going to eat here somewhere."

"We have reservations for half-past eight tonight. I was quite serious, Saber. Dress appropriately, of course. I would be happy with you wearing nothing but that lovely red towel, but the Pearl does have a dress code," Rik replied.

Saber nodded. *Man, I did lose time on Grimsey.* "Yes. Thank you. I'll see you at six."

"I think you should take a nap, Saber. Unless I am mistaken, you tried to out-drink the local fisherman and lost while on Grimsey."

"That's pretty much it, Ricky. I think I will take a nap."

"Shall I tuck you in?" Rik asked.

"After you take a shower, maybe." She blew Rik a kiss. "See you later."

She walked Rik out of her bedroom and waited until she heard the front door close before pulling on a nightgown and crawling into bed. *Another fucking ride on a puddle jumper. What is it with me and small airplanes?* And since when did Rik's dad get his own pilot?" With no one home to reply to her questions, Saber settled into her bed, grateful that she had the time to take a nap. Then reality hit. "Fuck! I have to work tomorrow!"

She reached over and set her alarm to go off in an hour.

She couldn't sleep.

Every time she tried to get comfortable, she found a new sore spot. She felt like *Indiana Jones* in *Raiders of the Lost Ark.* *Where doesn't it hurt? Try the eyelids. Or the elbow. Nope, the elbow hurts, too.* She'd banged it up against the Jacuzzi when she and Rik had done the nasty in the hot water.

She watched the minutes tick by on her clock, eyes wide open, comforter pulled up to her chin. It was broad daylight; birds were singing and she was sure that she heard the sound of grass clippers buzzing away somewhere.

She sprang from bed, exhausted from trying to nap, and flipped open her laptop. Her start-up music was "I Owe My Life to the Company Store." Appropriate. Sarcastic.

She clicked on her work email account. Somewhere high in space a satellite whirred to life. AlumaTrends had its own satellite. Flippin' prestigious sons of bitches running the show wanted zero delay time in their orders getting out to the front lines. She had ninety-seven unread emails. Not too bad.

She opened the one from her secretary in Seattle first. Always first. Secretarial emails come before all others.

It was her appointment and training schedule for the next day. The hard hats had arrived and were set up in Husavik—about an hour from Akureyri. She had two training classes to teach. Ten and Two. Thank God she didn't have to get up at the crack of dawn—whenever the hell that was in a land of twenty-four hour daylight—and drive a rental car into places unknown. If she left at nine, she'd make it in plenty of time.

Saber replied to the email with a "Confirmed" symbol her employers used to speed things up. No chit-chat via email at AlumaTrends.

She opened up the engineer's email next. He'd uploaded photos of the site. She'd never see it—as the job didn't require her to travel to the fairly inaccessible western fjords. That was hardhat territory. And, apparently, a sacred area to the Hidden Folk. The eager-beaver wanted to show off and gain admittance to the "pass-code" hand-off ceremony by wooing her with computer-enhanced images of before and after. Such a dick. Saber rolled her eyes.

Saber clicked the images into slide-show mode. The slide show began with breathtaking aerial photography of the wilderness to be dammed and flooded to provide electricity for the smelter. Under the photo a small caption read: *Western highlands. Mapped by Ice-Age (beta).*

Saber clicked on the next photo. It was an overview of the area to be affected by the dam and smelter. Iceland's Grand Canyon would be partially submerged, a major river channel flooded and re-routed, and thousands of acres of undeveloped land would be submerged.

The wound at the base of her throat began to twitch. She rubbed the spot and pulled away fingers stained with blood. "Damn it!" Saber swore. She stood to get a tissue and collapsed as a rush of dizziness overwhelmed her.

SHE SAT ASTRIDE GISLI, sliding her mound over his shaft. Her wrist was against his lips. He was taking her blood. She watched as a trickle of blood made a little rivulet across his bearded chin. A stream of red in a sea of blonde. She pulled her wrist away from his lips and pressed her mouth against his, tasting her own saltiness.

He reached between them and positioned his member for a nice drive home. Saber pulled herself upright and began squat-thrusts atop Gisli. "I need to quit my job," she whispered—the comment not seeming odd or out of place at all. "What they're doing is wrong. What I created for them is wrong."

"You need to stay and change their minds," Gisli replied. He grabbed Saber's hips and manipulated the depth and speed of their union.

"I can't," Saber replied breathlessly. "I'm just one person."

Gisli held her hips firmly against his own, not allowing her to move. The torturous agony of not being able to work out her blossoming orgasm forced a low, guttural moan from her throat. "Let go!" she begged.

"Promise me you'll change things. *A great human revolution in just a single person will help achieve a change in the destiny of a nation and, further, will cause a change in the destiny of all humankind,*" Gisli quoted. He thrust his hips up, causing Saber to cry out again.

"You're killing me, Gisli. Please," Saber begged. "Let me come."

"As powerful an orgasm as you have now, so shall be your desire to change the course of AlumaTrends. Do you understand?" he asked.

"Yes. Yes. I understand." Saber moved furiously atop Gisli as he released her hips. His vice-like grip had pinioned them together like solder to iron, but released, she rode him for all he was worth. She reached her right hand between her legs and caressed her clitoris against his shaft as she climaxed. Her fierce up and down rocking motions pulled him off a moment later. He moaned and dug his fingertips into her thighs as he poured hot into her. She collapsed onto his chest. He pulled her head up to his mouth and slipped her newly pierced ear between his lips. As she trembled against him, he bit open her physical souvenir of crossing the Arctic Circle, and fed.

SABER AWOKE ON HER bedroom floor, again in a puddle of drool and freezing cold.

She dizzily pulled herself to her knees. It was five-thirty. Morning or afternoon? She had no idea. The sky looked the same no matter what time of day it was. She smelled potatoes cooking on the stove, their starchy odor wafting about the house like a poor man's perfume. Evening. Kristjana is making supper. All righty then.

Saber gingerly rose to her feet and moved to sit down on the bed. The scatter rug on the floor was stained with blood. She felt her ear. Yes, it was bleeding. She looked at her wrists. No bite marks. It hadn't been real.

She reached between her legs and winced. Hard, fast sex. Only hard, fast sex could leave her that raw and tender. "It was freakin' real. Goddamn Icelandic faeries are messing with me!"

Saber ran her hands through her hair and gripped two handfuls forcefully holding them out like bat wings. "Faeries? What am I thinking?" She sighed and bent her head down to her knees. *Rik must have snuck in here and did me while I was out, the shit. Yes—that's got to be it. He couldn't wait until we were on that puddle jumper flying across the Icelandic tundra.*

She headed back to the shower for a quick rinse then dressed for dinner. Her teal silk East Indian-style pantsuit with the long duster and nice gold brocade flats. She wore a thong and strapless bra so that the straps wouldn't show through the delicate woven shoulder decorations. She pulled her hair back and secured it with a scrunchie the same color as her suit. She quickly applied some cosmetics, making sure she repacked what might get smeared if she and Rik had dessert first.

RIK FELT REMARKABLY ill. He stroked his thighs, feeling only his own warm, after-shower flesh, but knew, in gut-wrenching truth, that he was actually stroking the flayed skin of a man long dead and buried. He did not wish to disobey his father. But he did not wish to fulfill his mission as a witchling prince and kill the lovely Saber.

He scraped his fingernails along his hip, hoping to pry away the Necropants in their illusory state. He succeeded only in creating a gash across his own flesh. He watched in horror as the blood beading to the surface was suddenly sucked back inside.

Rik turned and vomited into his waste bin.

Nábrók rippled against his skin, creeping and scurrying around like an errant flea or louse.

Feeling a panic attack coming on, his chest tightening and brow perspiring heavily, Rik curled up into a ball, and wept.

He didn't pray. He hadn't been to church since his confirmation. He had given very little thought to heaven and hell and those who rule them.

As he lay under his duvet, nauseated and frustrated, he came to realize that there must truly be a God, for his father—*his father*—was the Devil. How else could he have bade his only son to wear dead man's trousers? And commit murder for the sake of Iceland's industrial revolution?

I will kill myself before I kill Saber, Rik thought. *Nábrók* tightened its punishing grip around his privates. Rik gasped and brought his knees up to his chin as he writhed in agony. Even his thoughts had to be censored or *Nábrók* would crush his testicles in an unholy vice-grip. It would take one swift action, without too much forethought, to be freed. But before he killed himself, he planned on making love to Saber again. And again. He'd have to kill himself before she did at any rate—should she discover he wore the Necropants. What woman wouldn't be repulsed and horrified to have been violated by a dead man's member? Yes...better he kill himself before she had the chance.

HE ARRIVED PROMPTLY, driving Daddy's nice German car. Wearing a dark blue suit, he looked much older than his eighteen years. "You ready to fly with me, Saber?" he asked.

"I think you already took a trip around the world today, huh?" she replied, sliding into the passenger seat of the car.

"What?" Rik asked.

"I had low blood sugar or something. I passed out on my bedroom floor. You are one naughty boy, Ricky. Doing a girl while she's down like that. If you wanted to play out a little rape fantasy, you could have asked," Saber replied.

"I'm not sure I understand. Are you saying we had sex? In your room?" he asked.

"Yes."

Rik slid into the driver's side and closed the door. "I do not consider rape worth fantasizing about. Six black women in a hot tub, maybe...but never rape. And although I was hoping to make love to you tonight at some point, I have not yet had the pleasure for today."

"I guess I dreamed the whole thing," Saber replied, ignoring the sneaking suspicion in her gut that the entire incident had been, indeed, real.

"I am flattered that you dream of having sex with me. I'd pull over this car and feel my way around that lovely blue silk you are wearing if we didn't have dinner reservations on the other side of the country."

"Keep your hands on the wheel there, buckaroo. Plenty of time for love later. How big is your father's plane?" Saber asked.

"The museum owns a Cessna Skyhawk SP. My father said I may commandeer it for the evening."

"That's a little bigger than a puddle jumper, isn't it?" Saber asked. "It seats four passengers comfortably, right?"

"Yes. And there is a privacy screen between the pilot and the cabin," Rik replied. "And the back two seats fold down."

"Are you trying to get into the mile high club, Ricky?" Saber asked.

"Yes. And there is something else I want, too," he replied.

"What's that?" Saber asked.

"I'd like you to blow me as I drive the car. Put your head in my lap and give me oral pleasure."

Saber wasn't sure how to reply. "We are having a purely sexual relationship, right? I mean, giving you head in the car won't make us engaged in some Icelandic custom I know nothing about?"

"I want you for your body, Saber. Nothing more. I'm eighteen and until a few days ago, was a *wirgin*. I applied myself quite diligently to my studies in school and did not make time for girlfriends. I would like to have as much sexual experiences as possible with you before I move away to go to University. Please don't be offended if I do not wish to marry you."

Saber withheld a burst of laughter. "Can you move the steering wheel up a bit?"

Chapter Three

She hadn't done it since high school, but walking the tight rope of giving head to a driver of a vehicle, in traffic, and not getting her prom dress sticky could be done. Saber knew to watch for signs of eruption. The hand on the stick shift, clenched and with white knuckles. The increase in speed. The shallow breathing of the driver. "Pull over," she demanded. There was no way she was going to let Rik orgasm while maneuvering a round-about.

He pulled into the parking lot of the Hagkaup grocery store. He put the car in park and leaned back while Saber finished the job.

He wasn't sure how he would subdue her. Would he strangle her as she sucked him, or beat her to death outside the car? What about the tire iron? He should have brought a knife or strong rope. His hands would have to suffice. Of course, it would go better for him if he just slit his own throat first. Killing Saber would just make her angry. The rage of a black woman wronged by a man—Rik was sure any pain the Necropants could dish out would be less traumatic than what Saber could muster—even dead.

Saber grabbed a conveniently placed box of tissue at the exact right moment and stroked Rik's orgasm into it. "Any other things you want to try out?" she asked, sitting up. She rolled down the window and tossed the tissue out. She then opened her purse, popped a breath mint into her mouth and reapplied her lipstick.

Rik had not yet said a word. His breathing had slowed some, but Saber was fairly certain his heart rate was still a tad too high for him to drive.

"That was incredible," Rik whispered. *And I'm so sorry to have deceived you! Please forgive me. I want you so desperately. I am an inhuman cad.*

"Quite credible, I dare say," Saber replied. "Here, have a *Tic Tac* and let's get going."

Rik zipped his fly and set off toward the airstrip. "Thank you."

"My pleasure, Ricky. Anything to warp the youth of Iceland. Incidentally, what kind of soap did you use to wash up with? It has an interesting aroma."

Rik choked. "Interesting?"

"Yeah, interesting. Not in a bad way, Ricky. It's just not how you usually smell." Saber paused. "I know, I'm weird. I have a keen sense of smell. You usually come off smelling like Ivory soap. Today you have more of an earthy scent."

"It's because I am a man now. You saw to that—and my father has also given me more responsibilities. Adult responsibilities. Some of them of quite a serious nature. The errands he wishes to send me on are of questionable legality—but that is the nature of business, from what I understand."

"I see. Well, don't get too sucked into the underworld of big business, Ricky. Been there. Done that. And I'm getting out while my soul is still intact," Saber replied.

THE AIRPLANE WAS *fine*. "Is your father wealthy or just plain filthy rich?" Saber asked, buckling herself into one of the very nicely appointed leather seats.

Rik shrugged. "I suppose he is. He has a position of some authority in Iceland and is well paid for his services. He's a consultant of sorts. I'm finding out new things about my father every day. He is quite the busy body, traveling all over Iceland for his research."

"Well paid for his services? The man has use of a private jet for his son to use on a date. That's more than just well paid!"

"Powerful men need powerful allies. My father has friends in high places. And someday, so shall I."

"Taking over daddy's business?" Saber asked.

"I have no skills as an archeologist or curator. I'm going to run AlumaTrends someday." He paused and turned his head to look directly into Saber's eyes. "I'm going to be your boss in a few years."

Saber raised her eyebrows. "What happened to journalism?"

His eyes widened as he caught an odor of goodness emanating from her. He cringed. Damned Old One. Foul being of light. "I am destined for greater things. My father is going to have me apprenticed next year. I shall attend University and learn the business side of the aluminum trade."

"All these changes in two days' time. You're growing up awfully fast, Ricky. I'm thinking of looking for a different line of work, anyway," Saber replied. "My presto-change-o act for the last forty-eight hours."

Rik laughed. "Why?"

"Well, I've decided not to hand over the passcode for my computer program to AlumaTrends. What they're doing is wrong. I mean...it could be done well—but how they want it done is wrong. Jobs are great—but the environmental impact is horrendous. Do you know they plan to flood the great rift in the western fjords? I can't believe that I was so blind. And the trouble I'm going to be in—I'm sure to get sued. I'm giving my resignation tomorrow."

"You took the transfer from Seattle knowing what the job entailed, did you not?" Rik asked.

Saber didn't like his tone. She found it scolding and accusatory. "You know, I never gave it much thought until recently. I wanted to get away from Seattle, have always been fascinated with Iceland, and when the opportunity to travel for my company arose, I leapt at the chance. I now have a one-year consultant contract with AlumaTrends, for better or worse. I think it's going to get worse. Worse by my own hand. But, I think the corporate planners are wrong and I'm going to say something. They can't beat the passcode out of me. They don't own something I've never written down. It's intellectual property. And I've decided it's not for sale. I need to read my contract again. There must be a way out. If not, I'm in for some major legal fees."

"The new plant will open up new jobs to many Icelanders now languishing due to the restraints on the fishing industry," Rik replied.

"That's true—but the cost is so great and dear. I saw photographs of area to be flooded. It's magnificent. AlumaTrends should develop a new energy source—or tap into a very old one—to power their plant. That, I would help with."

Rik fiddled with his window shade as he replied, "Hydrogen fuel cells, solar power, wind, and tidal power have been considered."

"I think they should run a pipeline to the hot springs outside Isafjordur and use steam to generate the electricity to run the plant."

Rik nodded. "By damming the river and flooding part of the canyon, the electricity can be generated much sooner than by building a new steam channel."

"Cheap electricity versus the destruction of Europe's largest wilderness expanse. I feel like instructor for a group of physicians about to begin systematic pregnancy terminations on a group of virgins."

"If you don't train the workers how to use their computer-guided system, someone else will," Rik replied. "You might as well accept your lot in this and do your job as well as you can."

"Or I can bloody-well quit."

"You'll lose your work visa if you leave your job. Do you want to return to Seattle so soon? What makes you so environmentally-minded all of a sudden?"

"I'm a good consultant and trainer. I could find work. And I guess I'm just having a change of heart. It's allowed, you know. The more I learn about what AlumaTrends wants to do to this country, the more sickened I am."

"It's not your country," Rik replied softly.

"Iceland gets under your skin, Ricky. I belong here. That doesn't mean I want to give up my US citizenship or change my name to Nathansdottir—but I love it here."

"I think you have been seduced by the *Huldufolk*, Saber. You speak as if you were one of their worshippers—always making love to the grass and rocks. When you were on Grimsey, did you meet anyone in particular? Perhaps someone as white as a ghost?" Rik asked.

"I met the inn keeper. A personal assistant to the manager of the Grimsey Trust and some crazy dude watching polar bears. And that was half the population."

"Grimsey Trust." Rik said the words with obvious contempt. "The administrator is an adversary of my father."

"Why?" Saber asked. She glanced out the window of the plane. They were passing over the Myvatn Lake area. Blue and green rolling hills and thousands of cinder cones and calderas dotted with little white flecks—sheep—looked extremely surreal from above.

"The Trust wished the Necropants immediately destroyed when it was discovered. The Trust sent henchmen to stop my father. My father, however, had the authority of the government to excavate the site and the Trust had no right to interfere," Rik replied.

"Bad blood there, huh? Is the Trust responsible for the theft?"

"No. The Trust is not responsible."

"You found the culprit?" Saber asked.

Rik nodded. "After a fact, yes. I know who has the Necropants. They are safe, and being used as they were intended. Unfortunately for the wearer, I might add."

Saber closed her eyes tightly. The motion of the plane had sent her stomach rumbling. "That's sick. You told me yourself that a witch wants to wear them to become master of the universe or something."

"Or something, yes," Rik replied.

She peered out the window. "Look, we're over Askja. It's steaming!"

"It is an active volcano. It could erupt at any time," Rik replied.

"Like you?" Saber asked. She took his right hand in hers and placed it over her bosom. "How much time do we have before we land?"

"It takes only an hour to fly across the whole of Iceland, Saber. We have about forty minutes," Rik said. He traced his fingertips over Saber's peaked nipples.

"So what's stopping you?" Saber asked. "Wanna?" She slipped out of her silks and turned slowly before Rik, displaying her lovely push-up bra and thong. "You like?"

He nodded. "You have the marks of a blood-sucker, Saber."

"I fell down an embankment."

"No, I think a *wampyr* made love to you and made you his," Rik said. He wasn't undressing.

Feeling rather vulnerable and losing the mood, Saber replied rather tersely, "I'm nobody's bitch, baby."

Rik reclined in his seat. "I think you have had another Icelander between your sweet thighs. Come closer. Let me examine you."

"Examine me?" Saber asked.

Rik cupped the rise in his suit pants. "I have the instrument to examine you right here." He unzipped his fly.

"Yeah, baby. Now that's what I'm talking about." Saber stood, straddling Rik's legs. His dick was in his right hand and his left was busy between her legs, making ready his pathway.

As he stroked his member, relishing the warmth of Saber's mound against it, he felt *things* go a bit dry. A small silver flask in his pocket shifted and began to echo his heartbeat. He needed a nip to keep things fresh. He shook with pain as he realized that his body was truly, no longer his own. As long as he wore the breeches, he acted on their behalf.

He reached his right hand into his pocket and deftly unscrewed the cap. *Is it better to be the right hand of the devil than to be in his way?* He lifted the container to his lips. *It is not better.*

"What have you got there, Ricky?" Saber asked, moving against his still-prying fingers.

"Nothing you would like. It is a very strong drink. Made from traditional ingredients."

"Lemme have some," Saber begged.

"I think not. I will let you have some of this, however." He pulled her onto his lap. "Ride me, Saber."

Saber backed away. "No baby, this time you do me." She dropped to her knees and bent over the seat, displaying her round bum.

Rik laughed and moved into a comfortable position behind her. "Ah, we are hounds tonight, are we?"

"Yeah, come on, Ricky. Do it."

He moved the thin thong aside and touched the head of his penis to her anus. Saber moaned. "Take the elevator to the next floor, mister."

Rik laughed and teased them both by pressing the head of his shaft just barely into Saber's vagina.

Saber moaned. "Hand me that flask, Rik."

Rik looked at his capped flask, containing the precious blood he needed to keep the Necropants from going dead-flesh on him. "No, Saber. I'm sure you will not like it."

He pushed his way into her.

Saber moaned and reached for the flask. She took a swig before Rik could stop her. She held the liquid in her mouth for a moment, then began looking around for something to spit it out into.

Rik pulled away, panicked. "Saber, don't spit it out! Not on my father's leather seats. Put it back. Put every drop back into the flask!"

Saber withheld a gag reflex as she dribbled the contents of her mouth back into the flask. "What the hell, Ricky? Is this blood? Whose?"

"It is blood. It is an initiation for University. Do not be alarmed. It is from a sheep, not a freshman."

"Jesus Christ, Rik. Where can I get cleaned up?" she asked. *God damn. I should really go after older men. College fucking boys!*

"I said you would not like it. Next time, please do listen to me. There's a small restroom near the cockpit," Rik replied.

Saber rose, dramatically waving her arms. "God damn college boy pranks. Make the new kids drink fucking sheep's blood. Jesus Christ!" The plane hit an air pocket and she toppled back onto the seat, spilling the flask, sending the blood everywhere. "Shit. I'm sorry. I'll go get some towels."

Rik choked back tears. He could not weep over spilled blood. Of course, he needed the blood to retain the illusion of the Necropants into flesh. Soon enough, they would begin to tighten and whither, taking him with them as they crumpled into dust.

As Saber used the restroom and searched for clean bar towels, Rik picked up the flask and drained the last drops of blood from it. He blotted up what he could with his handkerchief. Unless he could squeeze blood from the hankie later in the evening, he was going to have to do the unthinkable and take blood from a living being. He wondered if he could drink his own blood. Would that not suffice?

SABER DID NOT RELISH tight, confined spaces—such as airline restrooms. Give her the size of an Amtrak handicapped restroom for traveling, any day. She had her grandmother's curves, and those curves did not like being cramped or confined when using the facilities one bit.

She washed her hands and tried to do a little acrobatic maneuver to clean up down below in case she decided to give Rik another go. Was he worth it? A boy who carried a flask of sheep's blood? Yeah. He was a good man. He'd make a great lover. But the blood ...Jesus Christ!

She poured a drop of liquid soap onto her fingertip and touched it to her tongue. "Grandma says that's for the potty mouth," she whispered. "And to wash away that awful taste." The soap burned and tasted nasty. What was her world coming to when she was punishing herself with soap in the mouth for using bad language? *Maybe I am possessed by some goody-two-shoes, fabulous blonde vampire, polar-bear watching son of a bitch. Damn. More soap needed.*

She looked into the mirror, wishing she'd brought her handbag in with her. She smoothed back her unruly curls and wiped the lipstick that had dried in the corners of her full lips. Using a tissue she blotted the smeared eyeliner.

"Fabulous, as always," she said to her reflection. The plane hit more turbulence and the cabin lurched. Saber reached for the sink and held on, her eyes closed. She felt herself being pulled into a downward spiral. A sensation she recognized as having occurred all-too-recently. "Damn. Not again," she whispered, before succumbing to the vibrations over taking her.

His blonde head was at her mound, and his tongue was going to town. Saber clutched his head, finding it difficult even to breathe as the first wave of orgasm struck.

She came forcefully, holding his face to her body for dear life. When she relaxed, he didn't. She felt a twinge of pain on her vulva. He'd bitten her again. "Damn vampire pixie!" Saber swore. "Get out of my head!"

"The name is Gisli, and I am not a pixie."

"Why do you keep haunting me?" Saber asked. "I mean, can't a lady use the restroom without being bled by a vampire these days?"

"We are connected through your blood, Saber. I need you to set in place a plan to protect Iceland from developers and the sacred lands of the Hidden Folk."

"What about the sex? You keep sexing me."

Gisli smiled. "I am enjoying that part of the connection, very much."

"I'm not! Admittedly, I saw you and wanted to jump your bones, but darling, I'm not sure you're even real!"

"I am real. But we are no longer two beings. We are one."

Saber tightened her jaw. "Get out of my head, Gisli. Get out of my head and let me be about my business. I have a fucking country to save here, after all." She sat down on the closed toilet. "That's not me, is it? That's what *you* want me to do. You want the country saved from some Necropants wearing bitch witch and I somehow got trapped in the middle of your scene."

"The Necropants are working their magic on the witch as we speak. Though this witch is not inclined to acts of violence, *Nábrók* are all-controlling," Gisli replied.

"So make her take them off. You're a vampire! Don't you have super human powers?" Saber asked.

"I'm not that kind of vampire. I am a shifter. I am able to share a host body and move that person to do good acts."

"Good acts, my ass. You've messed me up, Gisli." Saber reached out and squirted another drop of liquid soap onto her finger. "Look at this! I feel compelled to wash my mouth out with soap whenever I swear. That's you, isn't it? Freakin' good-guy vampire. Only in Iceland!"

Gisli laughed. "It is my influence, yes. As I said on Grimsey, I am polishing your life. But truly, Saber, I am only tapping the goodness already in you. Now, please, listen to me carefully, for you are in danger."

"What? The witch in her Dolce and Gabbana dead man's trousers is going to fly by on her broomstick?"

"You keep referring to the witch as *she*. You do know, in Icelandic, there is no word to describe a male witch, so the term is used for both sexes," Gisli replied.

"Warlock. In English, we call them warlocks."

A knock on the restroom door startled Saber out of her inner-communion with Gisli. "Yes?" she replied.

"I would like to use the water closet before we land, Saber," Rik said.

"I'll be out in a minute," she replied.

Saber closed her eyes again. "Gisli? You there?" she whispered. No response. Saber unlocked the door and stepped out. Rik smiled politely and entered the cubical before she'd even fully crossed the threshold. "Gotta go, huh?"

She strolled back to her clothing and dressed. "Gisli?" she asked again. Nothing.

Saber belted herself into her seat, glancing nervously out the window—for signs of black hats and broomsticks.

Chapter Four

Saber felt pretty skanked-out after the blood fest on the plane. She had dinner at a three-hundred-dollar a plate restaurant coming up with a hot red-head who wanted to do her every which way but loose, a flippin' shifter-vampire moving in her veins and she'd grown a damned conscience over AlumaTrends' business practices—all this led to one conclusion: she needed a drink. Maybe tying one on would relieve her of her Icelandic demons. Of course, they could probably drink her under the table. This was Iceland, after all.

The Pearl—*Perlan*, with its revolving restaurant built under a sparkling glass dome built over hot water tanks atop a hill, was probably the most unusual venue to eat fish in all Europe. Surrounded by pleasantly wooded footpaths leading to a natural geothermal beach, the place had both a magical and high-class feel to it.

Rik and Saber entered through the atrium, below the dome and above the hot water tanks. The wax museum was closed, but they could still peer through the bars at the magnificent statues of Vikings and early Icelanders. "Yo, Ricky...that your great-grandfather over there?" Saber teased.

"Considering we can trace our lineage back to the year one thousand, chances are *wery* good, it is." The dryness of the Necropants was causing him some discomfort. "Dear one," Rik began. He wanted to tell her. Wanted desperately to disobey his father and tell Saber the entire, sordid tale. The words escaped him. "I'm afraid I must use the closet again, Saber. Would you be all right if I leave you for a moment?"

Saber laughed. "I'm not going anywhere, Ricky. Unless Witchipoo shows up on her VvroomBroom, I'm good."

Rik squinted and leaned forward, an obvious look of confusion on his face, "Witchipoo?"

"Never mind. I'll wait here by your wax homeboys. You hurry back," Saber replied.

Rik kissed her quickly on the cheek and headed off in the direction of the public restroom on that level, the Necropants tightening and chaffing him with each step.

He brought his hand to his mouth as he walked across the level. He dipped into a stall and bit the fleshy part of his palm beside the thumb. He drew blood and pulled enough for one good swallow. It had no effect on the Necropants.

He unzipped his trousers and pulled his briefs away from his body. The flesh of his abdomen and privates had grayed and wrinkled. His penis seemed to have shriveled into nothingness. This would never do. Sacred vow notwithstanding, he could not go through life with the flaccid penis of a dead man. Not when he'd just learned how to use it properly! He stripped off his trousers and shorts and attempted to peel away the dead man's breeches. They held fast like a boot forced upon too small a foot. *Nábrók* twitched and tightened. Rik put the handkerchief in his mouth and desperately tried to suck the blood from it.

Nábrók twitched, tightened and pinched his member so hard he thought he would scream like a little girl.

Rik pulled up his dress pants and stepped out of the restroom, determined to hydrate *Nábrók* and figure out a way out of them without having to kill Saber, after dinner.

SABER SAT DOWN AND mentally called to Gisli. *This is no fun for me, you damned daylight vampire! I didn't sign up for this! I came here to …*

"To what? Make money? Drop the bomb on a great expanse of wilderness?"

Saber turned her head. Sitting next to her, was the blonde god. "How did you do that? Get from my veins to this bench?"

Gisli replied with a smile and sing-song tone, "Shifter."

Saber grunted. "I don't like this one bit. You tell me I'm in danger and then disappear. You live inside my veins like some kind of STD infection, yet make me mad with desire whenever I know you're around. And damn it, you've made me second-guess my whole life plan. I didn't come here to save the world, Gisli."

"No, you came here to save the western fjords from greedy developers. We'll take on the world next week," Gisli replied.

"So, who's out to get me? And why?" Saber asked.

"Saber!" It was Rik. "Come along, you must see the view from this side!"

Saber clenched her fists. *I am never going to figure out what's going on here!* Gisli had again vanished at Rik's approach. *Damn pixie!*

THE SECURITY GUARD didn't know what to do. He'd never had trouble of this kind at the Pearl before. In fact, other than the occasional tourist shoplifting a trinket from the souvenir shop, his job was fairly uneventful. He placed his strong arm around the shaken woman. With a heavy German accent pervading her attempt to speak English to the guard, she described a horror he found hard to grasp. Had she been drinking? He sniffed her hair as she sobbed. No. There was no alcohol on her person. He cautiously peeked under her shawl. Sad brown eyes looked up at him, and a little tail wagged slightly—below what clearly looked like a human bite mark.

"I put his little leash around the pole and used the restroom ever so briefly. When I returned, he was gone. My little boy was gone."

A miniature dachshund. Her little boy. The guard rubbed his beard thoughtfully. "And then you found him behind the potted plant?"

"Yes. With the horrible wound on his back!" the woman sobbed.

The guard stroked the red-coated dog's smooth back. "He seems fine, but you had better take him to the animal hospital on Langholtsvegur."

"Someone bit my dog! He is not fine!"

"I have alerted the police, Mrs.—one will be here shortly. I must go examine the area where you dog was injured now. Will you be all right alone for a moment?" the guard asked.

The woman nodded and held her dog closer to her chest. There was a very miniscule ring of blood on the shawl above the dog's hind end. Who would bite a dog? He thought immediately that a small child had stumbled across the hound and teethed upon the friendly little beast—but the bite marks were too large for a child. It was an adult. A lunatic. A lunatic at the Pearl. Or perhaps one of the Hidden Folk—the Yule Lad, *Bjúgnakrækir*, the sausage pilfer, came six months early and thought the little wiener dog was food. The guard chuckled. That would be something, indeed.

RIK SEEMED TO HAVE a skip in his step that made Saber believe she was about to experience more than just fine dining. As the ascended the staircase, he smiled and chuckled to himself, sometimes whispering in Icelandic. "You're a happy boy tonight. The restroom offer more than usual?"

Rik slipped his arm around Saber. He'd made a conscious decision to tell his father to piss off. He didn't want to be a witch prince. He may have been born to it, but his heart was not cut out for such duties. That decision was now well accepted.

Nábrók lashed out and scratched at him like a scourge. Rik held onto the railing and coughed as the maitre d' welcomed Rik with open arms. Rik regained composure and embraced the maitre d'. "Saber, this is the Captain of the Pearl. He is an old friend of the family."

"Enchanted, Miss Saber," the Captain replied, bowing slightly. "Please, let me show you to your table."

Saber had been wined and dined a time or two. She'd once dated a Japanese businessman who jetted her to Tokyo for a weekend. And that rich Texas bank executive—well, he'd been fun, but so damned conservative! However, the Pearl and the man next to her took the cake. Never in her life had Saber entered a revolving restaurant overlooking one of the cleanest, most pollution-free capitals in the world. On a clear day, you really can see forever in Iceland.

"This is amazing," Saber sighed, unable to take her eyes off the vista as her table boy pulled out her chair.

"Perlan is noted for its interior and exterior views," the Captain replied. "Your server will be with you in a moment. May I offer you a traditional aperitif before dinner?"

Saber looked across the table at Rik with a glance that clearly said, it isn't sheep's blood, is it? Rik laughed. "Thank you. Yes."

Blue glass goblets and silvery-gray linens graced the tabletop. Fresh lupines and roses were on each table and huge cut-glass chandeliers added to the ambiance as the summer sun struck them making little rainbows on the ceiling. "Is that the geothermal river down there?" Saber asked.

Rik leaned forward to get a better look. "Yes, it is. See the trees? Ten thousand saplings were planted. From Alaska. Hardy little trees used to harsh climates. The Perlan has magnificent grounds."

A typically beautiful young woman with bright blue eyes and insanely white-blonde hair approached the table. She was breathtaking. Robert Ripley had it right when he said he'd seen some of the most beautiful women in the world in Iceland during his travels.

"Gott kvold," she said politely, passing a menu to Saber, then Rik. "Tonight we have a very special menu. For starters we have seafood soup with vegetables and shellfish. Our second course is chicken liver mousse with bacon foam on focaccia biscotti. Choices of main course tonight are grilled breast of chicken with herb polenta and tarragon sauce, grilled John Dory with oyster mushrooms and bok choy, roast fillet of lamb with mustard, herbs and rosemary sauce, or tenderloin of beef bourginonne with butter fried asparagus and root vegetables. Sauce Béarnaise is served with all main courses."

"John Dory?" Rik asked.

"It is a fish from Australia. We have it flown here in tanks so that it is very fresh," the waitress replied.

Rik laughed. "This is Iceland! We're on an island surrounded by fish and you fly it here from Australia? This is truly the most magnificent restaurant in the world."

The waitress didn't reply. Saber chuckled to herself before ordering. Had she heard it all before? "Well," she began, "I've had enough of sheep for one night." She cast a sideways glance at Rik. "And the last thing I want to do is energize my brain by eating fish, so I'll have the beef."

"I'll have the same. Can I have my beef cooked very rare?" Rik asked.

"Of course, sir," the waitress replied.

She walked away, the large menus under her arm. Saber giggled. "She told us everything on the menu? Why's she toting those things around with her?"

"She's just doing her job. Something we all must do," Rik replied.

Saber wondered if that damned vampire pixie was listening. "Yeah. Only I'm rewriting my job description come tomorrow. I can't, in good conscious, continue earning six figures a year for a company that is going to destroy," she waved her arms at the horizon, "all of this."

"I wish you would reconsider," Rik replied, knowing he was only mouthing the words his father wanted him to say.

A police officer in his crisp blue uniform strolled by with the Captain. "I wonder what he's looking for," Saber remarked.

Rik turned in his seat so that no part of his face could be seen by the someone passing the table. "I wouldn't know."

Saber reached across the table and tapped Rik's arm. "Yes, you do. I can tell you're fibbing, Steinrikur Vidarsson. Tell me what's going on."

He turned to face Saber. "I am innocent."

"No you're freakin' not," Saber replied.

DINNER PROVED TO BE a near religious experience. It was hard to make polite conversation as one was experiencing an orgasm of gastric proportions. Dessert nearly sent her over the edge of decorum. White chocolate Crème Brule. To die for. Worth dying for.

They'd conversed little during their meal. Save for the moans of foodie ecstasy, there was little to say.

Saber leaned back in her chair, sipping her coffee and almost wishing for another serving of dessert. She looked out the floor to ceiling concave window. The geothermal stream called to her.

"I wanna go down there, Ricky," she said. "Let's go skinny dipping."

"In Iceland that is not such an event as it is elsewhere in the world. We are welcome to be naked as long as we are not touching anyone else's nakedness in public," Rik replied. He motioned for the Captain.

"Did you enjoy your meal?" the Captain asked.

"It was fabulous. Thank you," Saber replied.

"My compliments to you and your crew, sir." Rik passed a wad of Icelandic bank notes into the hand of the *maitre d'*. "We'll be leaving now."

"Thank you, Steinrikur. The staff will appreciate your generosity."

Rik extended his hand to Saber. "Come along then, the night is young and the plane will stand by until we are ready to leave Reykjavik."

"I have to work tomorrow. I can't stay out too late or I'll lose my edge and not be able to tell the corporates where they can stick their drilling devices," Saber replied.

"You must have truly been possessed by, what do you call it in America…a tree-hugger, while on Grimsey. You are not the same, Saber."

"You want that money-grubbing bitch back, huh?"

"I want the Saber who supported industry, yes. You must ask the spirit haunting you to step forward so that I can question his motives," Rik replied. They took the elevator down.

"Can't a girl have a change of heart?" Saber asked.

Rik pressed her against the glass wall of the lift, stroking her ribcage and hip with is strong right hand. "I like your heart how it was. Saber, I want to make love to you, again. I want to taste your orgasm."

Saber giggled and allowed Rik to nuzzle her throat—an area she'd been shy about sharing since Gisli put the bite on her. "I already had dessert, Ricky."

He licked the bite marks left by the Old One. He could smell the breath of antiquity on Saber. It made his stomach churn. "But I know you, you are wishing for more white chocolate. Just as strongly as I wish to devour more dark chocolate."

"Well spoken, Rik. But we're fogging up the elevator, baby. Tuck that monster of yours away until we get lost in that little forest of ten thousand trees, hmmm?"

Rik and Saber strolled hand-in-hand along the tidy white stone path leading from the Perlan, through the trees, to the natural hot water stream.

Rik's lower extremities began to itch. He'd not taken enough blood to keep the Necropants flexible and they were rebelling. He was sure he'd traumatized that poor dog for life.

It was wrong, the constraining Necropants and his desire to bite house pets. However, he had to keep the breeches happy—for now. *Keeping them happy*, was apparently, a necessary evil. Rik felt repulsed by his own thoughts. *Diabolical* was not his style.

The Necropants constricted. Painfully. He winced with each step as his penis became encased in a vice-like grip and tendrils of pain shop up his legs.

All right. All right. Rik pictured his thoughts traveling down his body to his legs where the Necropants would hear and release him from the stranglehold. *I shall do what I need to do. What has been commanded of me by my father. My way.*

THEY WERE ALONE BY the banks of the sulfuric stream. Steam rose from the water and its absolute clarity startled Saber. *So pure is Iceland. So very pure. I cannot spoil it. Enola Gay is not going to drop the bomb this time 'round. No way. I'm done.*

Rik slid his arms around her from behind. He was hard. She could feel his potent erection pressing against her backside. "My, oh, my. We're ready that quickly, are we?"

"You make me hard, Saber. Just looking at you. Your touch. Your scent."

"Ricky, you are becoming a fine young man. Who's been teaching you how to say sweet nothings, anyway?" Saber teased. She turned in Rik's arms and kissed him. "Let's get naked, huh?"

Giggling like school children they stripped and waded into the steaming waters. Saber dropped to the riverbed and stretched out. Her bosom peeked out from the slow, shallow current. Rik waded to her side and reclined next to her.

"This is heaven," she said softly. "Except for the smell."

"Sulfur," Rik replied.

"Rotten eggs. It's stronger over where you are. Can you tell?" Saber asked.

"Saber," Rik said softly.

"Yes?"

"This," Rik said. He reached one hand between her legs as his mouth found hers. He caressed her clitoris from its sheath and inserted two smooth fingers into her. His tongue flicked against hers in rhythm to the movements of his fingers. Her hips responded. He could make her come this way, or he could climb atop her, pin her, fuck her, and drown her into unconsciousness.

He chose the former.

Nábrók chose the latter.

Saber responded to Rik as he rolled atop her. He placed one strong arm under her neck to hold her head above the flow as he entered her. Fast, furious. He thrust deep and hard, seemingly caring only about his own pleasure. Saber tried to shift her weight under him, to encourage him to slow and make each pass against her swollen clitoris count—but he wouldn't have it. This act was for him. His pleasure. She'd been there before. She hated selfish men.

Rik didn't slow his momentum one iota, but crushed harder against her, his right forearm under her neck and then his left hand over her throat in a chokehold.

Saber fought against him, striking at him with closed fists, bringing her knees up, twisting her body to get him off. He didn't budge. He kept on pouring into her as she suffocated.

The sky went black.

She lost sensation in her arms and legs.

Her lungs were on fire and she could taste vomit in her mouth.

With one final lucid thought, she called his name. *His* name. The pixie that had been doing her from the inside, out. *Gisli!*

Her right hand moved down Rik's hip, her fingers intertwining in the ties on the pants, now balking at staying hidden. She yanked and snapped the ties.

Rik yelped and released his death grip. He felt it like it was his own flesh. As if she'd reached into his gut and pulled.

Saber pulled again, this time completely unlacing the ties.

She raked her fingertips across the burn mark on Rik's hip, drawing blood. His skin peeled away under her nails.

He rolled away, turning to examine the wound. She'd done some damage. The blistered flesh was open and weeping.

"What the hell are you wearing, Rik?" Saber asked.

Rik looked down. The Necropants had seeped from his own flesh and looked very much like some monstrous theatrical prosthetic for a Pan or Satyr.

Saber coughed and rolled onto her knees, then pushed herself to her feet. "I know what those are. You're wearing the Necropants. You're the fucking witch! You son of a bitch!" She lunged at Rik, striking him. "And you put that thing inside me? You let me put that thing in my mouth? What's the matter with you?"

Rik tumbled backward as Saber came at him like a pit-fighter, fists flying and knees going for anyplace that would hurt.

She got one good solid blow in with a right hook. Dazed, Rik's head hit the bank.

"You son of a bitch!" Saber spat. "Screwing me with a dead man's dick. How could you?"

She wasted no time in stripping Rik of the Necropants. The gruesome drawers pulsed with a heartbeat of their own in her hands. "These are nasty!" She called out, "Gisli!"

Rik coughed blood. "Gisli?" He tried to lift his head, but was so stunned he could not.

Saber waded to the opposite shore and slipped on the Necropants. "Now who's wearing the pants in this family you fucking jerk?" She heaved upon the shore as the Necropants adjusted to fit her sexy ass and long legs.

"Take them off, Saber."

She turned. It was Gisli. Brighter than the midnight sun and twice as gorgeous. "I called you an hour ago! I'm over here fighting with a damned witch trying to bugger me with fucking dead pants and you take your flippin' time getting here. I'm so tired of you screwing around inside my head it's about damned time you showed up in the flesh! You are in the flesh, aren't you?" she exclaimed.

"Take them off," he said again.

"Not a chance, mister. If that piece of work can screw me wearing these nasty drawers, then I intend to do the same to him. I cold-cocked the bastard. Just watch me figure out how to get this thing hard and I'll give him what-fucking-for!" She slapped the flaccid penis of *Nábrók*.

Gisli approached, a hand extended to Saber. "No."

Saber stomped her foot like a three year old. "Why the fuck not?"

"Because you forgive him."

"I do?" Saber asked. "I do? What do you mean I forgive him?"

"You will. We need him. Take off *Nábrók*, Saber. Give them to me." Gisli slid upside Saber, allowing her to use his weight to hold herself steady as she pulled off the Necropants.

"Against my better judgment," she said handing off the Necropants. "Now what?"

"We go to Myvasveit. There is an entrance to the realm of the Hidden Folk. They will take *Nábrók* and destroy them. With their destruction, and your persuasiveness on the morrow, Iceland will be safe," Gisli replied.

"What about him?" Saber asked, nodding toward Rik.

"He, and his father, will pay for their bad deeds, in time. Rik is much more valuable to us alive and in full possession of his faculties. Therefore, please do not batter him about the head again. We need him intact—especially right now."

"Why?" Saber asked.

"It's his plane."

Chapter Five

Gisli helped Rik into the Cessna and fastened the boy's seatbelt. Rik was both mortified at failing to do his father's bidding and for agreeing to do it in the first place. And for being beaten up by a girl. "I'm likely to be in a great deal of trouble when next I meet my father," he said. "You don't understand. I was born to serve his purpose. I am some sort of prince among the witches."

"Yeah, like that's more trouble than you'd be in if you'd managed to kill me," Saber replied. "My grandmother down in New Orleans taught me a thing or two about coming back from the dead, you..."

"I'm so sorry, Saber," Rik continued. "I was not going to kill you. I wanted you unconscious so that *Nábrók* might believe I'd killed you as my father had commanded of me. I would never have let you die, Saber. I was looking for a way to free myself of the breeches."

She slapped him across the face. "Oh, yeah, like that make everything better!"

Gisli stayed her hand. "Saber, I know you are angry. You've been through a lot. But know this, you are changing the face of this nation, and when you leave, you will need good men to step up and following in your footsteps. Ice-Eye has significant applications for predicting earthquakes and changes in ocean currents. Your program is going to revolutionize early warning systems all over the world. All you have to do is, in your fine, vocal manner, tell AlumaTrends what their new direction is. You are the backbone of the company, Saber. They will listen to you. They will be compelled to listen. Someday, Rik will work for you, not against you."

"No dam. No smelter. No jobs," Rik moaned. "Even before my father assigned me to run his terrible errands, I wanted the plant built."

"Steinrikur, you have a bright future helping to protect our wilderness areas. You can become a good friend to the Hidden Folk and be praised by the Old Ones for all time. Not many men have had this honor."

"My father is going to kill me," Rik replied.

"Your father is pawn of another, more powerful witch, and when *Nábrók* are destroyed, that witch will lose much power of persuasion. No more children will be initiated into the coven of the western fjords and most certainly, no more young Icelanders will be branded when it is time for their service to the coven to commence. The witch hunts of Iceland's past are over—now, instead of burning their bodies, we will burn goodness back into their hearts."

"You don't live with my father," Rik replied.

Gisli shook his head. "Eventually you will convince him that his path is not one lined with dollars and aluminum ingots."

"You're going to have to do some convincing my way, too," Saber replied. She wandered toward the front of the cabin, muttering to herself. "Vampires! Shifters! Boy witches who wear dead pants. I didn't sign up for this! And damn it, I broke a nail kicking the shit out of Rik!"

IT WAS A TWO-HOUR DRIVE, way past midnight, with a trek through fly-ridden terrain to reach the stone circle. "That's it," Rik said. "My father had me stand within the circle. A mist surrounded me and held me fast while he marked me. He called it Satan's Breath."

"It is nothing more than a steam vent in the grass. But, the Hidden Folk are strong here, and they ride up the steam to the surface," Gisli replied.

"Why can't we just burn the Necropants?" Rik asked.

"Because they're magic," Saber added. "Even I know you have to fight fire with fire. And I don't even believe in this shit. I think I'm unconscious somewhere and this is all a freakin' bad dream." She paused. "To destroy magic, you've gotta use magic. Right, Gisli?"

"Right, Saber," Gisli replied.

"It's nice to have you out of my head for awhile, man. I thought I was losing it." She went off of a tangent, not really expecting Gisli to reply. "Witches who drink blood are draugur and draugur are enemies of the Old Ones, who are vampires," she began.

"And Shifters," Gisli interjected.

"And Shifters! And I'm just some fine looking bitch who happen to smell right or something and got invaded in so very many ways by warring factions." Saber swatted at the flies. "I hate bugs! Now, hurry up and leave those damned drawers in the circle or something so that we can get out of this bug-infested sulfur pit!"

Gisli took Saber's arm. "Magic doesn't have to be difficult. It is that simple. We leave the Necropants, turn our backs, and walk away. Unlike the last time when we sealed them up in stone to be eaten away by time and tide, there is no escaping the underworld. They'll come to no evil purpose in the hands of the Hidden Folk."

"Unless a Yule Lad shows up in town wearing the pants next Christmas, that is," Rik replied.

"The Yule Lads wouldn't do such a thing." Gisli placed the Necropants carefully inside the stone circle arranged on the grass by Vidar. "They have shoe fetishes, any way. They do not want pants. Only your shoes."

"I have not placed my shoes in the window to receive a gift from the Lads during Christmas since I was a little child. I did not believe in the Yule Lads," Rik said.

"Ah, but I'm sure they believe in you. Let's go. Do not look back and do not speak of this after tonight," Gisli replied.

Rik walked away from the circle, sobbing. "I bit a dog. I bit a little dog at Perlan. The Necropants were growing unhappy and I bit a little dog."

"He's lost it," Saber commented.

"He will weep with remorse and from withdrawals from the power of *Nábrók*. But he will be fine."

"What about me? It's my head on the chopping block when I show up for work today," Saber replied.

Gisli slipped his arm in hers. "You will be fine, too."

"Am I going to have withdrawals from you?" she asked.

Gisli laughed. "I'm not going anywhere."

"What about Rik?" Saber asked.

Gisli smiled. "I'll share."

Epilogue

S**ix months later**

Saber finished marking a paper with bright red ink and slipped her glasses onto her desk. A gentle knock at the door stopped her from nodding off. "Professor Evangelista?" a voice called from behind the rippled glass.

"Yes, come in, Hafdis," Saber replied.

Hafdis Finnbogadottir, assistant to the Dean of Information Technology, stepped inside Saber's office. "Your car is waiting. Are you ready to be the first American woman to address *Althingi*? You are about to take part in a political action dating back to the year nine hundred thirty."

"It feels good, Hafdis. Very good. What we're doing feels good. Signing a compact to protect Iceland's wilderness is right. I've worked hard to get this on the table."

"And the agreement with AlumaTrends to build a steam pipeline and turbine windmills is revolutionary. Americans helping Iceland—without having to bomb us first. I'm so very proud," Hafdis replied.

"Is Rik in the car?" Saber asked.

"He is. He looks very handsome. He says his father is doing much better, too."

"Kristness Mental Health Facility is remarkable. I'm glad Dr. Gunnarsson is recovering from those awful delusions he was having," Saber replied. She straightened the nameplate on her desk before exiting her office. The Dean of Information Technology for the University of Iceland, at Reykjavik can't have a messy desk now, can she?

"It is truly miraculous that Rik has taken his father's illness so well. They were very close," Hafdis added. "I'm sure your attention has helped him find his way, too."

Saber smiled. She paid Rik attention, all right. Forgiveness was working for her. "Well, I'm off to make history."

She touched the scar at the base of her throat as she walked out of her office. It pulsed with a life-force she'd grown accustomed to, and cherished. It was all good—all of it.

The threesomes weren't bad, either.

DARRAGHA.COM
BOOKS WITH SPICE AND SASS
DARRAGHA
FOSTER

www.ingramcontent.com/pod-product-compliance
Lightning Source LLC
Chambersburg PA
CBHW022027150726
47990CB00002B/847